Freaks
Like Us

Also by Susan Vaught

Freaks
Like Us

Susan Vaught

BLOOMSBURY

NEW YORK LONDON NEW DELHI SYDNEY

First published in the United States of America in September 2012
by Bloomsbury Books for Young Readers
www.bloomsburyteens.com

For information about permission to reproduce selections from this book, write to
Permissions, Bloomsbury BFYR, 175 Fifth Avenue, New York, New York 10010

Library of Congress Cataloging-in-Publication Data
Vaught, Susan.
Freaks like us / by Susan Vaught. — 1st U.S. ed.
            p.   cm.
Summary: A mentally ill teenager who rides the "short bus" to school
investigates the sudden disappearance of his best friend.
ISBN 978-1-59990-872-4 (hardcover)
[1. Mental illness—Fiction.   2. Missing children—Fiction.   3. Love—Fiction.
4. Mystery and detective stories.]   I. Title.
PZ7.V4673Fr 2012   [Fic]—dc23   2012004227

Book design by Nicole Gastonguay
Typeset by Westchester Book Composition
Printed in the U.S.A. by Quad/Graphics, Fairfield, Pennsylvania
2 4 6 8 10 9 7 5 3 1

*To the many young men and women who have given me
the privilege of working with them over the years.
I admire your courage and strength.*

Freaks
Like Us

∾ PROLOGUE ∾

NAME   *Jason Milwaukee*
SUBJECT   *Algebra II*
DATE   *September 6*

Some days life makes more sense than other days.

The algebra problems in front of me might as well be *Moby Dick* or *A Tale of Two Cities* or *A Separate Peace*. I've had to plow through all three of those since I got to high school, and I didn't like any of them.

I'm told I don't think like other people, and I'm pretty sure that's true. Not that I could explain it, even if I tried, but I always try, so—here's this.

I talk great in my head, but I suck out loud, and sometimes because there's so much racket, I'm not good at staying on track or explaining what I see, or maybe it's that I'm not good at figuring out what I'm really seeing so I can put words to it.

It's because of the voices.

When I turned eight and went swimming over at Noodle Creek, I met up with the wah-wah voices. That's how I remember it happening. Not that the voices started or grew or popped into my head or came on because of some bone-deep soul-clawing trauma. It was more like they started whispering and I started looking for them and I sort of found them or met them or whatever, though I wouldn't call them friends.

Wah-wah-wah-wah.

That's how they sounded at first, one or two of them talking, then three or four, then five or six, and that's all they said, like swishy mutters I couldn't quite make out or understand, words that weren't words and heartbeats that weren't heartbeats and roars that were mumbles and mumbles that weren't really anything at all. It's hard to explain, and then it gets too loud, and—

Sorry.

Don't worry. I don't usually see things, like, *see things*, you know? Not unless it gets really bad. Mostly I just hear the voices.

Do the algebra test, stupid. That's Bastard. He's been pretty loud lately.

You'll fail, you'll fail, you'll fail, says Whiner. She's always loud, and she sounds like she's singing.

Don't bother, says one of the No-Names. And, *Maybe you should try,* says another, and *Maybe you shouldn't try,* says a third one. *Maybe you should try. Maybe you shouldn't try.*

Shut up, shut up, shut up, sings Whiner.

Bastard and Whiner and the No-Names. There have been others over the years, but this bunch of voices sticks around even when I take the fuzzy pills. They get quiet and they get distant sometimes, but they never really go away. It's like having five or six radios in my brain, all tuned to different stations, with a few extra radios playing nothing but static.

Sometimes when I really jump the track, I start rhyming things and then laughing at the rhymes, but I don't mean to. Sometimes I think scary, wacked-out junk, too, and I definitely don't understand stuff the same way everybody else does, or so Drip and Sunshine always tell me, only Sunshine makes it sound like a good thing. Drip just makes it sound, well, drippy. Like a guy who's allergic to the planet has so much room to pass judgment on anybody else.

We're all six years old and we're standing in this new school in this new class and we're here because other kids make fun of us and we can't get our work done and maybe we were bad and this one kid he's tall tall basketball tall and skinny and his nose runs like everything and he's got a hanky and he wipes it and he sticks out his hand and says I'm Derrick Taylor but my brothers call me Drip and the girl she's got this long dark hair and long dark eyes and this quiet little smile and she plays with the little gold locket on the thin gold chain around her neck and she doesn't say anything but Derrick Drip says her name is Sunshine Patton

*and my mama says her name really is Sunshine it's not a nick-
name and she's shy* and then he listens like he can hear her even
though her lips don't move and he says *Sunshine wants to be best
friends can we all be best friends*

$-1 + (y+7)/(2y-6)$

What?

That's the next problem on my algebra test, and don't
look at me, because I've got no clue. I think algebra should
be optional, but nobody ever listens to people like me.

$SQRT(x-6) \star SQRT(x+3)$

SQRT? Seriously? There's no place for squirts in math,
and what am I supposed to do with a $\star$? What does anyone
do with a $\star$?

There isn't even a stupid equal sign. Math's supposed
to have all these rules, then algebra breaks them, and that's
supposed to be okay.

Drip's working on his test and sniffing and using his
tissues and he's way taller now than he was in first grade,
like big-long-basketball-tall but he couldn't bounce a basketball without breaking his toes with it. Sunshine can.
She can do gymnastics and run fast like a cheetah and she's
good at math, too, but she hates English, and right now
she's at her desk between me and Drip, and she's not writing because she's already through with her test and she's
keeping her arms over it so Linden Green and Roland
Harks can't see it.

Way back when we were six years old and decided

to be best friends, we should have known then that we'd end up here together, the three of us, Freak, Drip, and Sunshine, riding a short bus and hanging out in a single self-contained classroom labeled SED.

That's Severely Emotionally Disturbed, for you long-bus people.

SED is different from other special-education classes, even though we all ride the same bus. The people in SED class, a lot of us can do regular schoolwork, just not in a regular classroom. Most of us can learn just fine, only our alphabet gets in the way. There's ADHD (that's Drip) and just ADD without the H. There's MDD and BPD and GAD. When I first started school, I was GAD, Generalized Anxiety Disorder, because I was nervous about everything and the doctors thought that was my disorder, but really it was just the first part of a bigger disorder because now I'm SCZI. Schizophrenic. That's my alphabet now. Sunshine's our only SM, selectively mute, only she's not selectively mute with me and Drip, but we don't tell anybody because Drip's mom was right all those years ago. Sunshine's shy. She doesn't much like other people, and Drip and I take care of her, or maybe she takes care of us. Doesn't matter. We're not ratting her out.

We're okay, mostly, our bunch of alphabets. That means we try to do our work and we don't beat on each other and even if we have problems sometimes, we get our meds changed and come right back and start over with $(2x-6)(7y-8)$ and we still don't beat on anybody.

Then there are the other alphabets. The Linden Greens and Roland Harkses of our self-contained world. CD—conduct disturbance. ODD—oppositional defiant disorder. APD—antisocial personality disorder.

Beating on everybody, that's what most of them do.

SQRT(−8*4)?

Forget it. The bad alphabets don't try problems like these because they won't, not because they can't. My mom the colonel says the school system shouldn't put people like me and Drip and Sunshine in the same classes with those other alphabets, but the school system says if you're an alphabet, you're an alphabet and you're in here, and I live with Dad, not the colonel, and Dad isn't a colonel. He used to be a lieutenant in the army and now he's a captain at the fire department. Dad says the system is the system, and some battles aren't worth fighting. The colonel's all about battles and bucking up and holding it together, but when Dad told her to stop fighting the school system about where to put which alphabets, she dropped it. For the most part, my mom and dad get along even if they aren't married. I'm lucky that way. I've got Dad during the week and the colonel on the weekends, three weeks in the summer, and every other holiday when she's not deployed. Sunshine's never met her real dad and Drip's dad isn't allowed to come within five hundred feet of him or his mom or any of his four older brothers. So, see? I am lucky.

"I need your paper, Jason," Mr. Watson says.

Linden mumbles, "Freak."

Freak, says Bastard, and Whiner and all the No-Names pick up the echo, so it's *freak freak freak freak freak freak freak* from different directions and different sides and different volumes and some of those radio stations not coming in all the way but I don't really care. *Freak* doesn't hurt me any-more. I embrace *Freak*. I am *Freak*.

Mr. Watson waits. He's used to me taking a minute to do what he says.

Do you think he'll be nice Sunshine asks and she's squeezing her locket and staring at this new teacher this Mr. Watson who showed up our first day of tenth grade and he doesn't look a lot older than Drip's biggest brother but I guess he couldn't be a teacher if he didn't finish school and get his degree but seriously with that baby face and the wild scraggly curly hair and big eyes he looks like a scrawny caveman who bit a live wire but I say yeah he looks pretty nice and Drip says I don't know because he's littler than Linden and how can he make Linden and his boys do anything and Sun-shine says it's not like the teacher gets to hit anybody anyway so we leave it right there and Mr. Watson gets to stay nice or probably-nice and later Sunshine announces everything will be okay and everything will be okay because Sunshine said it

I hand in my paper. Mr. Watson takes it and smiles at me and he still looks like an electrocuted caveman. When he doesn't shave, it gets worse. I do what I can to smile back, but I'm never really sure if I'm smiling because my alphabet makes smiling hard and lots of times I think I am but I'm not. Mr. Watson takes Drip's test and Drip smiles because Drip smiles at everybody even when he shouldn't. Mr. Watson takes Sunshine's paper. He tries to catch her eye but she looks down fast because Sunshine still doesn't talk to him. It's only been two years. Sunshine needs a lot longer than two years to get used to people, especially guy-people, except for me and Drip.

You're cute Jason because she calls me Jason even though every-body else calls me Freak even Drip but Sunshine calls him Derrick which you'd figure anyway last year she says you're growing muscles and you're cute Jason with your thick brown hair and those big brown eyes but I tell her the colonel says my hair looks like a mop and my face is starting to look like a bristle broom and she says the colonel doesn't know everything and sometimes I wonder if maybe just maybe I count as a guy to Sunshine because I don't to anybody else not really me or Drip either we're here but we're just here to most people but to Sunshine maybe we're more than here maybe even better than here and that would be really really nice if it was true

"It's okay, Sunshine," Mr. Watson says, and he keeps standing at her desk and she stares at the floor and keeps her fist around her necklace, a golden locket she never opens, her cheeks red as pain and cinnamon and she wants him to go away. She wants him to go away but he doesn't, and now I'm wanting to make him go away and I know Drip wants to make him go away, too. People just don't understand how hard it is for Sunshine.

Make him move, you stupid coward, Bastard mutters.

Don't, don't, don't, sings Whiner.

The No-Names are still stuck on *Freak, freak, freak.*

You enable your friend. That's not one of my wah-wah voices. That's what one of my doctors told me, one of the ones who gives me my fuzzy pills and asks about my life and my friends and I tell him about Drip and Sunshine. I see him once every three months when stuff is good and he gets letters from my school and the colonel talks to him and so does the captain, so he always knows what's going on, or at least he thinks he does. *You enable her and you help keep her sick.* And I say okay but I'm not doing anything different because Drip and Sunshine and me we've got secrets we won't tell anybody, even him or our parents or you or anybody else. We've got promises to each other and nobody can make us break them. *Don't talk for her*, the doctor insists. And I say okay because okay's a good word and it's easy and the doctor moves on and Sunshine's still safe and nothing has to change.

Later, after school, we're walking through "bus alley," a narrow sidewalk between the two rows of buses that pick people up, past all the long buses, heading toward the short bus way up in front, and nobody looks at us. Most people our age ride with friends or have their own cars, but our parents haven't let us get licenses yet. Drip would run right up somebody's tailpipe and Sunshine would be too scared to turn on the car. I'm not sure I could drive, either, but sometimes I want to try.

You can't drive, you idiot, you stupid, worthless piece of trash. You can't, you can't, you can't. Maybe you could? I think you could. No, you can't.

Can you guess which voices said which things? Yeah. Bastard, then Whiner, then the No-Names. They always seem to go in order, then all at once, like one big run-on bunch of yammer. I usually don't bother paying attention to who says what. It's distracting, especially when it's bad. It's not bad right now, though.

"I want to go see *Lands of Eridor* when it comes out," Drip says. "Can you go with me Saturday, Freak?"

I yawn because the last class, American History, made me too sleepy for words. "The colonel won't let me. My doctors say no fantasy movies."

"You get to read fantasy books," Sunshine says. Her hair looks blue black in the warm afternoon light. There's the slightest breeze with a hint of cool and fall and colored leaves, and I can almost see those yellows and reds and oranges in the depths of Sunshine's dark eyes.

I shrug, trying not to trip over my feet as I gaze into her eyes. "Movies are different, I guess."

"Ask the captain," Drip says. "That's what I say. We can go during the week."

He's got a point. The captain's a lot less uptight than the colonel. Usually.

"Hey, pretty girl." The voice comes from behind us, and we all three wince and walk faster, because it's Roland, and if it's Roland, then Linden's not far behind him. They used to ride the short bus before they got cars, so they know where to look for us.

"Pretty girl," Roland calls again, and we don't stop and we're not planning to stop, but Linden Green steps out from between the last long bus and our short bus, and he's sort of smiling and then he waves, so we stop.

Green, Green, just plain mean. That's the rhyme I made for him once when I was getting a little more nuts than usual. He's seventeen and officially in tenth grade, though in alphabet-land we're really "ungraded" and all together, ninth and tenth and eleventh and even twelfth, the last grade, like Sunshine, Drip, and me. Roland's taller than Sunshine and me, and he's got a lot more muscle than me and Drip. The way his dark eyes always look too bright with anger, and the way he keeps his dyed-black hair styled and the stupid look on his face, he could pass for a mobster extra, you know, the muscle thug who breaks fingers for fun and pleasure.

"Roland wants a word," Linden says.

You're stupid to give in to him, you coward, you piece of

junk. Green, Green, just plain mean. He'll break your fingers. He'll break your nose. Maybe he will. Maybe he won't. . . .

All the voices, all running together. No point in naming them now.

Drip cracks his knuckles because he's nervous, then has to drag out his tissues and blow his nose. I wish I had to blow my nose. I wish I could do something, because I hate stuff like this. Sunshine's already shaking, and I want to take her hand, but that won't help us with Roland.

He comes around to stand next to Linden, and he's not looking at Drip or me, just Sunshine. She's not looking at him, even though lots of girls do. Roland has charcoal hair and clear blue eyes. He's the kind of guy who would be handsome if he weren't evil. No, seriously. It's not that I'm crazy, okay yeah, I know, I *am* crazy, but so is he. In a different way. Roland is a whole different alphabet, and I wish he didn't have to spell himself out near me or Drip or especially Sunshine.

"Pretty girl," he says to her with that too-gentle tone he always uses, trying to get to her, to get her to notice him and look at him and I'm afraid one day he'll be talking to her like that as he hammers bamboo shoots under her fingernails and tsk-tsks and tells her she made him do it.

Sunshine doesn't lift her head. Her right hand drifts up and grabs her locket.

Roland has probably memorized the part in her hair by now, because that's all she ever does, show him the top

12

of her head while she squeezes her locket as if it can cast spells to make him go away.

"I just want to talk to you," Roland says. "Maybe grab a burger? Would that be so bad, pretty girl?"

Say something, you chicken. Don't let him scare her like this. Tell him to quit. Tell him she doesn't belong to him. Chicken, chicken, chicken. He's scaring her. He's not really scaring her. Maybe you're not a chicken . . .

Roland takes a step closer to Sunshine, and if he lifts his arm, he'll touch her, and here in bus alley it's so narrow and cramped we can't go sideways. We can't go forward because of the bad alphabets, and if we run, they'll catch us.

"Give us a break," Drip mutters, because he can mutter and get away with it sometimes because he's got big brothers and the bad alphabets know that.

"Stay out of this, Dripmeister," Roland says.

"Dripmeister the Stretch. Stretch the Drip." Linden sounds like my voices, but he's not, even though he might as well be.

Sunshine just stares at the ground and shakes. She lets go of her locket. Her fingers flutter toward mine and I really, really want to hold her hand but I like my teeth and I'm scared of getting my nose snapped and Bastard's right, I really am a total coward.

"Just a burger, pretty girl." Roland is trying to sound charming. He might be succeeding. Maybe other people don't see him as the kind of guy that'll make an evil empire with minions one day. Maybe that's just me and the wonked-out way I think, which gets worse when I'm nervous and I'm getting nervous now.

Sunshine doesn't think Roland is charming.

Hold her hand, all my voices say at the same time, only Bastard calls me lots of names in the middle of it.

"Hey, you!" The shout comes from behind me and Drip and Sunshine, and it scares us, and we all jump, but then I realize it's her brother, Eli Patton.

On any other day, at any other moment, that might be its own problem. Eli's nineteen, the oldest kid in the school, and he's only five foot six, but that gives him sawed-off-runt syndrome really bad, and it's worse because he looks like a mug shot. He can't help it. That's how he's built, square and short with bristly coffee-colored hair, big ears, and a perpetually pissed-off expression. He's even got tattoos on his fingers, *PAIN* on his left hand and *HOPE* on his right. He got them during the two years he spent in juvenile for assault and battery.

Linden gets all puffed up and swaggery as Eli jogs up the bus alley and pushes between Sunshine and me. Eli ignores him and focuses on Roland with a growly, snarly "You buggin' my sister again? Because I know you're not."

All of this just makes Sunshine shake harder but I still don't have the guts to take her hand as Eli and Roland glare at each other and Linden does a lot of trash talking but keeps his distance.

Coward. You should hate yourself. Girly-man, girly-man, girly-man. Are you really a man? You're not really a girl. Maybe you are . . .

All the voices, all at once. It doesn't even matter who says what.

And maybe because there's an actual felon involved, our lazy driver, Mr. Poke—that's his name, not making it up, I swear—finally comes down from the short bus and starts hollering about the principal and the police and detention, and Roland and Linden give Eli a last set of not-so-friendly gestures and melt off between the long buses.

"You okay?" Eli asks Sunshine, and she doesn't look at him, but she nods. His Dumbo ears flush a dark red, and he touches her on the shoulders, just barely touches her like a brother checking on his sister, but she flinches like he's scalding her, so he stops and says he's sorry, then, "Karl will be here in a second to take me to the probation officer. Want us to give you a ride?"

Sunshine shakes her head so hard I'm surprised her brain doesn't fall out her right ear.

"Okay, okay," Eli says, sounding sorry but also a little pissed, which is pretty normal for him. "I'm just—you know. Covering the bases and making sure everything looks okay. Don't get stressed."

Covering the bases. Making everything look okay. That's me echoing what Eli said, not my voices. Because that's what we're always doing, right? People with problems like mine and Sunshine's and Drip's. We have to cover the bases. We have to make everything look okay.

"Let's move," Mr. Poke says.

"Everything will be fine," Eli tells Sunshine as he gets out of our way, then he says something about Karl leaving town as soon as he drops Eli off and Eli picking up dinner after his meeting, and Sunshine doesn't say anything.

Sunshine barely gives Eli a glance as the three of us cover ground in a hurry, jogging up the bus steps, then heading to our assigned seats at the back.

Yes, we have assigned seats. It's a short-bus thing.

I realize I'm breathing heavy, and Drip's blowing a lot of snot, and Sunshine's just sitting in her very back seat not looking at either of us.

"Sorry," I tell her, and I think I'm meaning about not holding her hand but she probably thinks I'm meaning about Roland bugging her again.

She shrugs and does a little shake with her head, which is Sunshine for *No big deal, just give me a minute.*

Drip and I glance at each other, then out the bus window. We see Eli getting into his and Sunshine's stepfather's car. It's a newer model, but still big and gas hungry and shiny black. As for Karl—Mr. Franks—he's got thin sandy-brown hair and a mustache and lines around his eyes. I don't like Mr. Franks, but I don't want to think about that because it doesn't really matter who I like or don't like, so I shift my attention back to Sunshine.

Her china-white skin's getting a little color to it, at the neck and ears and chin, which is all I can see of the front of her, the way she's bent over, but that's good. It's normal for her. She's coming back to us an inch at a time, like she always does. Her fingers tap against her golden locket like she's counting. It's small, not any bigger than the pad of her thumb, and the etchings have been worn smooth from where she rubs it so much. I've never asked her what's in it because it seemed wrong. She'll tell me if she ever wants to.

Sometimes I wonder, though.

The short bus starts up like it always does, except on really cold days, and it leads the bus wagon-train away from the high school.

Drip and Sunshine and me, we stay pretty quiet on the bus, which has kids from other alphabet classes, the kind for people who stay like little kids in their heads forever, so they're noisy, several of them, hooting and laughing and talking to Mr. Poke. About half an hour later, we get off the bus on Slide Street, also known as Apartment Avenue because of all the apartment complexes built like hives and warrens into the hillsides.

For a while, as we walk up the hill, we talk about homework and what we're having for dinner and what we're going to do about Roland if he won't leave Sunshine alone, but that's all we ever manage—talking about it. We never *do* anything, because we're alphabets and alphabets are disorganized, and besides, nobody listens to us anyway.

Then Drip heads north toward the upper-scale Crestview duplexes where he lives, and Sunshine heads south toward Hilltop (her town house complex has a pool), and I walk straight across the street, covering the hundred or so yards to the entrance to the decent Skymont apartments where I live with the captain.

I'm home by four thirty. Drip hits his front door by four thirty-three.

And somewhere between "Bye, Jason" and five o'clock, Sunshine Patton disappears from the face of the earth.

ONE HOUR

If bad stuff happens to the people you care about, you'll know. If bad stuff happens to the person you care about more than anything else in the universe, you'll definitely know. It's always that way in books, right? But what I'm thinking when the captain gets home around five fifteen like he always does is I'm crazy hungry and he's gonna make mac and cheese like he always does and I like mac and cheese but I'm tired of it and . . .

Stupid, you're so stupid and ungrateful, and, *Mac and cheese if you please, mac and cheese if you please,* and, *Maybe he will, maybe he won't, maybe he will, maybe he won't.*

Captain Johnson Milwaukee is a creature of habit, just like me. He's taller, but not by much. He's balding, and his thin hair is a mix of gray and brown. His uniform is black with silver buttons, and the patch on his sleeve and the badge on his chest have bright orange flames so people know he's all about putting out fires instead of chasing bad guys. He's slightly overweight, but I don't care and he doesn't care. What I like most about him is that he's relaxed and calm, and he's decisive in a quiet, confident way.

Yelling at fires doesn't put them out. That's one of Dad's mottos.

Act now, panic later. That's another Dad-ism.

When my parents got divorced, I was twelve and I got to choose, and I decided to live with Dad because it's just easier for two guys, and because his sayings help keep my brain straight, and because the colonel lives on base when she's not deployed and I don't want to live on base and I'm pretty sure the colonel would go crazier than me if she tried to take care of me every single day. The captain won't go crazy. The captain helps me stay as sane as guys like me ever get, so when he gets home and hangs his hat in its spot by the pole on the door, gives me a point-and-shoot gesture, winks, and says, "Mac and cheese," I go put the water on to boil.

I know which pan to use. I know exactly how much water to pour into it, and I know how to pretend I'm putting in the pinch of salt he wants but doesn't need because he used to smoke and his heart and blood pressure don't need extra problems. We're two guys living alone, and we've got this easy-cooking thing down to cups, teaspoons, and stir-in-the-sauce-and-bring-to-a-boil.

"Want some sausage in the mac and cheese tonight?" Dad calls from his bedroom, which is just off the kitchen in our little two-bedroom apartment.

"Sounds good." My voice is all flat even though I mean to sound light and who-cares or anything except flat or thank-God-not-just-boring-mac-and-cheese-again. The flatness happens because of my alphabet. Dad's used to it. He never gripes when my face and voice go blank. He knows why. The colonel's not so good with that whole acceptance thing.

I grab the sausage out of the fridge and pull off the wrapper before he pays much attention to the fact it's marked lean and healthy. When the colonel shops for us at the PX, that's what she buys, and I'm not arguing with her about it. I'm not arguing with the colonel about anything ever, if I can help it.

Dad heads into the kitchen wearing his jeans and a black fire department T-shirt that shows his paunch. The darkness of the fabric stands out against the simple color scheme of our apartment walls—white and white and more white. The cabinets are light wood and the flooring in the kitchen is light white vinyl, and all the energy-saver lights are bright, so the theme of light-light and bright-white stays unbroken. Dad doesn't smell like fire smoke or cigarette smoke, so I know he's not been doing anything dangerous today. The only scent in the kitchen is the wet-metal smell of water starting to boil, and that's when the phone rings.

It's bad. Whatever it is, it's your fault, you loser. It's awful,

it's terrible, it's awful, it's terrible, it's awful, awful, awful.
Maybe it isn't. Maybe it won't be. But maybe it is?

I ignore the voices as Dad answers, because they always say the same stupid stuff when the phone rings or the doorbell chimes or there's a knock or a registered letter. Fifty-one million people in the world with my alphabet, and I had to get neurotic voices. I guess that's better than angry voices or really paranoid voices. I have no idea how many types of voices there are, but mine usually run to the doom-and-disaster side of things.

Dad's standing at the counter behind me and the water's boiling. When I turn to glance at him, I see him looking at his watch.

"No," he says. "She's not here, Ada." His brown eyes flick to my face, then to his watch, and back to me. "What time did you get home, son?"

"The usual," I tell him, then process that he's talking to Ada Franks, Sunshine's mother. "By four thirty."

Dad's thick, dark eyebrows—which haven't thinned like his hair—do this funny pinch thing when he's listening and thinking at the same time. "Okay," he says to Ms. Franks, then to me, "Did Sunshine come home with you?"

"No, sir."

"Do you think she went with Drip, or did she say she was headed anywhere in particular?"

"We all left from the corner, same time we usually do, and no, of course she wasn't headed anywhere." Weird.

Sunshine should be home by now. Way past, in fact. And Sunshine never goes anywhere without me or Drip or her mom and sometimes her brother, Eli, because of the whole shy-and-doesn't-talk-much thing. Everybody knows that.

Stupid moron. You should have walked the girl home. You owe her that much, don't you? Owe, owe, owe the girl, owe the girl all daaa-aaay. Nobody owes. Everybody owes. Do you owe her anything?

"Jason doesn't remember anything unusual." Dad sounds matter-of-fact, but I catch the tone. The unsaid *you know what I mean*. Because, of course, I might not remember things right. I might think a little crooked.

I do think a little crooked, but I remember this afternoon just fine.

Don't I?

"What happened when you tried her cell?" Dad asks Ms. Franks, which isn't as strange as it might sound. Sunshine has a cell even though she doesn't talk on it ever, not even to her "safe" people. Her mom got it for the GPS locator function in case Sunshine ever got lost and couldn't make herself say or write her name or address for whoever found her, but she hates that phone and she hardly ever carries it.

"I see." Dad directs his frown at the kitchen counter. "It's in her room on her desk. Well. That doesn't help very much."

He keeps pinching his eyebrows, and I'm feeling weirder and wondering what's going on and maybe if once, just this time, Bastard is right and I should have walked Sunshine home. I've hardly ever done that, but after what happened last Saturday—

Don't get all different Jason please you have to be the Jason I've always known or the whole world will just blow up and I won't be able to stand it and I promise I won't be different and please and I'm saying yes okay whatever you want I'll give it to you but she's still crying and squeezing her locket and I don't know if she's crying because I know or because of what happened or if I don't know everything because when a girl cries what does anybody know but nothing nothing nothing and I wish she'd stop and why don't I know how to help her stop please please don't cry anymore Sunshine

—For a second, I'm stuck in *then* instead of *now* because time can do that to me, it can stop making sense, it can stop having the periods and commas and paragraphs and chapters that divide life into yesterday, today, and tomorrow or even a few hours ago.

She made me promise.

She made me promise I wouldn't say a word, that I wouldn't even think a word about it, and it turned into black clouds in my head because I promised I'd forget it and that was last Saturday. This is Monday. Saturday,

Sunday, Monday. I tick the days off with my fingers as Dad pinches his eyebrows and asks Ms. Franks if she's called here or if she's called there, and no she's not here and no she's not there and nobody's seen her since the bus, nobody's seen Sunshine in more than an hour and that's just not normal.

Piece of trash. Bastard's growling now, and somebody hit his repeat button, so he's doing it over and over with Whiner in the background singing, *Owe, owe, owe, woe, woe, woe* and the No-Names just keep whispering *Saturday* and *promise* in different tones, in different volumes. Some of them are loud.

"No, you don't have to wait," Dad says to Ms. Franks. "She's a vulnerable child. Her diagnosis—yes. Chief Smith won't mess around with any twenty-four-hour rules in a situation like this. If he's not there and any of the junior officers give you the run-around, you call me straight back." Then he stops again and pinches his brows so tight they make a salt-and-pepper V between his eyes. "Yes, you might want to call your husband and tell him to come back home as soon as he can manage it."

His frown gets worse. He starts trying to get words in, but he can't, and his hand pats the counter like he's trying to comfort Ms. Franks through the phone. He keeps saying stuff like "I know," and "We'll be there," and "Probably just some mix-up."

When he hangs up, he calls Drip's mom, who's just

getting home from work. Ms. Taylor checks with Drip, but Drip hasn't seen Sunshine, either, and Drip gets on his cell and starts calling his older brothers to find out if they've seen her, and I imagine each call like a pebble dropping into liquid air, making huge circles and ripples across our white walls and white floors and into other walls and over cars and across people's ears, and maybe one of those ripples will land on Sunshine and she'll start sparkling like a quest diamond in a video game. She'll be the thing on the screen that we all run toward and grab and hold, but in my own head it's not a pebble that drops into my mind as Dad tells me when each of Drip's brothers says no, no, no, we haven't seen her, we don't see her around anywhere, no, it's not a pebble that drops into my mind, it's a giant rock, it's a prehistoric meteor, and it doesn't drop into my mind, it explodes through my whole body, it craters my entire awareness, vaporizing the lake of my mind and wiping out everything for miles and miles and miles.

Sunshine—my Sunshine—

She's . . . missing.

"Son?" Somebody's got me by the shoulders and I'm trying to pull away, but I shouldn't, because it's the captain. I know this because nobody else calls me *son*, not even the old guys at school who call all the other male students *son*. I'm the one they don't want to claim. I'm the one nobody claims except Dad and the colonel and Drip and Sunshine.

"Come on, Jason." Dad doesn't shake me, but he holds me so tight I realize I'm shaking myself with all my twisting around. "Come back to me."

Freak, freak, freak, freak, freak, freak, FREAK, freak, FREAK—

The voices yell so loud I wish covering my ears would help but I know it won't. I don't hear the voices in my ears. I hear them in my mind. "Freak," I echo, seeing nothing but the meteor-scorched white, white walls and then slowly like it's being drawn in midair, the outline of my father, and he smells funny, like melting iron.

"I don't like it when you call yourself that name," Dad says, and he doesn't sound funny, and that's a totally Dad thing to say, so I'm pretty sure he's Dad and not some sudden iron-stinking demon.

"Freak's what I am," I mumble. "It's okay."

Old argument.

Name-calling hurts, Dad always says, *even when you do it to yourself.*

Name-calling doesn't hurt because *I do it to myself.* That's what I say.

The voices in my head get quieter, enough for me to breathe and think and see time in a straight line and see my father standing there with his fire department T-shirt.

He looks worried as he turns me loose. "What happened just now, Jason?"

"I . . . don't know." But yes, I do know. I flaked out. I

freaked out. I freaked out because I'm a freak. My own personal f-word sets off Bastard, Whiner, and the No-Names all over again, yelling and singing and whispering *freak, freak, freak, FREAK*, but I keep it together this time.

"Sorry," I say to Dad. "I guess I got stressed."

Dad studies me for a long second or two, then lets out a breath I didn't know he was holding. "You . . . absolutely sure nothing happened with Sunshine today?"

What does that mean? What does he mean?

Tell him nothing happened, you stinking puke. Lie to him. Or tell him it's your fault. Tell him you only wanted her to stop crying. It's her party and she'll cry if she wants to. Nobody wants to cry. Everybody cries. Do you cry?

It doesn't feel like nothing happened even though I know nothing did, but when the voices start, it's hard for me to keep track of *real* and *right now* instead of fears or pretend memories. I don't say anything to Dad because my brain gets stuck on the my-fault thing and wondering where Sunshine is and if somebody took her, and if somebody took her why they took her and why there have to be takers in the world to leave people like me with nothing.

". . . probably nothing, but in case it is something," Dad's saying as he turns off the pan that boiled dry, making everything smell like hell metal.

"What?" It's an effort not to shake my head, but rattling my brain doesn't stop the smell or the voices, either.

"We need to go to Sunshine's apartment," he says,

exasperated, like he's said it before already. "It'll be help-ful for you and Drip to tell me and Chief Smith and Sun-shine's mother everything you can remember about today. If Sunshine really has gone missing, then the key to what happened, to where we should look for her, might lie somewhere in the last couple of days—especially the last couple of hours."

The last couple of hours or days . . . oh.

But . . . no.

He can't mean *that*. That's a secret. That's our secret, mine and Sunshine's.

You piece of crap. It's your stinking fault. I told you you'd go to hell. Straight to hell. The devil's waiting for you, Freak. Freak, freak, freak. There is no freak. There's always a freak. Are you the freak?

Okay, not this. Not right now. When the voices get loud, and especially when they turn to heaven and hell, things are starting to get shaky. I don't need shaky right now. Sunshine doesn't need shaky.

It's hard isn't it when they talk so loud Sunshine says and it's last year again and things are still as simple as they ever get for us but she says I don't want you to have to go back to the hospi-tal because Derrick and I miss you too much and it's boring and I'm so sorry you have to go through it Jason and I tell her thanks because most people can't imagine but I think Sunshine can imag-ine because she has her own problems even if she doesn't talk about

them ever and sometimes I want her to but sometimes I'm scared
she will and I won't know what to do and I won't know what to
say and I'll let her down and I'll hurt her and

Did I hurt her?

No.

But . . .

Last Saturday is such a mess in my head.

No.

I promised. Don't talk about it, don't even think about
it, let it go, put it away because I promised and I always
keep my promises to Sunshine but maybe I should try
because this is an emergency and emergencies change
things but when I try my head gets louder and louder and I
can't stand it and I can't think and I can't see anything at all
but black swirly clouds and the clouds are talking and—

"Son, is there something you need to discuss?" Dad's
voice makes me jump.

"No. I—the pills." I rub my right ear and the sound
of my fingers against my skull eases everything for a few
seconds, everything but the horrible pound-hurt-pound
in my chest where my heart's supposed to be. "It's hard to
think sometimes."

Dad gives me a little smile, so I know I'm acting calmer
than I feel, which is good. I think. His smile doesn't reach
his eyes, and something flickers in the brown depths as he
studies me.

Monsters. Dad has monsters in his eyes. God, how stupid is that? Get a grip. Keep *a grip.*

"I know your medication muddles your thinking," Dad says. "And Chief Smith will understand. You just do your best. Let's head over to Sunshine's house. I'll call your mother on the way."

TWO HOURS

She looks like Sunshine.

That's about all I can think when I see Ms. Franks. Different last name because she's married to Karl with his stupid mustache. She's older, with shorter hair, and darker skin from lying in tanning beds—but she's got the black eyes, so wide and dark and deep they might be shards of the universe trapped in a person's soul.

She looks like Sunshine, sitting there with Chief Smith in his blue-and-gray uniform, writing on his notepad while Dad stands beside them and nods and watches and pinches his eyebrows. I'm sitting across from all of them and I'm being quiet because—

Sunshine would be here if you hadn't been stupid, if you'd walked her home, if you hadn't done bad things like you knew you shouldn't, you stupid ass. How could you be so stupid? Stupid

is, stupid does, stupid is, stupid does. Nobody's stupid. Every-
body's stupid.

—But Ms. Franks really looks like Sunshine, with her
petite build, her bird bones and bird fingers and the way
her bottom lip trembles and she looks to the side when she
talks. She's sitting with Chief Smith on the nice leather
couch in the nice hardwood living room of Sunshine's
very nice, very big three-bedroom townhome. We could
put three or four of my apartments in here. The whole
place smells like apples and that makes me breathe funny
because—

Your house smells like apples your room smells like apples I tell
her but you smell like honeysuckle it's in your hair and on your
skin and everywhere around you and she says it's my shampoo
but I know it's her it's really her, that she's made of soft yellow-
and-white blossoms with just that one drop of too-sweet honey
waiting inside but when I try to tell her that she laughs at me and
says no silly I mean it it's my soap but she kind of likes the idea
that she's made of honeysuckle flowers because she says you really
don't think like everybody else Jason and then before she starts cry-
ing really crying with that sobbing that tears me up inside she says
there's lots of times I wish I could think like you

—"We've checked the school, the bus," Chief Smith
says from somewhere far away. "We've done a first walk
of the route, and nothing's apparent."

And then his lips move because he's talking, but I'm

not quite hearing him or he's not making sense until the last couple of words, which are ". . . saw her."

And he's looking at me, and I've got no clue except to think that he's got even less hair than Dad, and the two of them look enough alike to be brothers.

"Sorry," I mutter. When I look at Dad, Dad nods at Chief Smith.

The chief of police is a decent guy, polite and nice most of the time, and he eats dinner at our house at least once a month, so he knows me a little bit. I know when he's being patient and when he's just trying to look patient, and right now he's halfway in between.

"I need you to tell me your day, Jason," he says, sounding like people always sound when they have to repeat themselves to me. "Start with getting to school, the first time you talked to Sunshine, and take me through the last moment you saw her."

"I got on the bus just after seven," I tell him, watching Ms. Franks sit with her hands folded and her chin trying to dip down and make her stare at the floor and she looks so much like Sunshine it actually hurts me like a chest punch. "Drip rode with me, but Sunshine wasn't on the bus, because her brother gives her a ride most mornings."

"Eli." Chief Smith makes his notes. "Got it. What did you and your friend Derrick discuss on the ride?"

"I don't remember what Drip and I talked about," I tell him, using Drip's nickname because to me it's his real name like Freak is mine, and it's not anything bad or to be ashamed of, being who and what we are. When you're an alphabet, you have to be real about the things you can be real about, since everything else is so complicated. "Something about *Quest Nine Thousand*, probably. It's a game we're playing. We got to school around eight, and—"

And she's waiting near the front door so quiet and turned away and almost invisible because I see her before Drip and my heart jumps funny and I leave him digging through his book bag to see if he forgot his English homework and I get to her first and her black eyes shine when she looks at me actually looks at me right at me and way down deep inside as she asks are you okay and my heart jumps funny again because I can't believe she's asking me that because I should be asking her that but she promised me and I promised her and whatever I need to remember it's all gone from my head because I promised and there's nothing but black swirly clouds where last Saturday used to be and then Drip's there and

—"And we all met up at the front door of the school, and we went to class." I try to smile but I probably don't because of my alphabet and—

Liar. You lying little piece of trash. Liar, liar, pants on fire. Not lying, just not telling. Not telling isn't lying. Not telling is lying. It's all a lie.

—"That's it?" Chief Smith's eyebrows are almost as

thick as Dad's and they look funny when they're raised up so high.

"My life's pretty routine." I shrug. "Nothing much goes different—not most days, anyway."

He makes me go through each part of the day, class by class. Yes, Sunshine had her homework. No, she wasn't upset about anything *that I'm telling you*, she didn't get in any trouble, no, nothing happened out of the ordinary *on Monday* and his face is starting to blur until it looks more and more like Dad's, and I have to glance at Dad to remind myself that they aren't the same person and that Dad hasn't disappeared or turned into something other than Dad, so Chief Smith can have his face.

Yeah, I know I told you I don't see things, and I don't, but sometimes I have trouble thinking about what I'm seeing. Everything can get weird, especially when I'm tense and I'm way past tense at this point and maybe yeah, sometimes I do see things.

Where is Sunshine? This isn't really happening, is it? I mean, she'll show up in a second, won't she? And where is Drip?

I wish he'd get here. I want Drip to come so badly it's almost like I can will it to happen, but the knock on the door that stops me from talking about the math test and how I hate negative numbers doesn't sound like Drip's bumpy thunder-pound. It's a crisp rap, exactly three knocks, exactly evenly spaced, and I know who it is before Dad nods to Ms. Franks and goes to open the door.

The colonel says a quick hi to Dad, then strides into Sunshine's living room with a younger woman trotting beside her and slightly in front like a medieval herald. The colonel's wearing her desert fatigues with a white T-shirt underneath barely showing through the collar. Her light-brown leather boots look dusty. She kisses the top of my head, then says something to Ms. Franks about what she's wearing, and sorry, training maneuvers.

The medieval herald stands silent, wearing dress greens that probably got pressed an hour ago. No training maneuvers for her. She's blond, young, looks uptight—but she does have bars on her collar. I rifle through what I know about rank insignias, and I realize she's a captain, so she's probably older than she looks.

"This is Captain Andrea Evans," the colonel says, and she doesn't say anything else about older-than-she-looks Captain Evans. At a gesture from the colonel, Captain Evans heads to the fringe of the room, near the front door, and just keeps standing there, quiet as can be.

Stupid witch. What's she doing here? She's probably just watching you because you're more stupid than she is. Stupid is, stupid does, stupid is, stupid does. Nobody's stupid. Nothing's stupid. There's no such thing as witches.

Before I can think much more about it, the colonel's on the couch beside Ms. Franks, and she's saying, "Do we know anything yet?"

Ms. Franks sits, hands on her knees, staring at the floor, and she shakes her head. Mom pats her hand, and I realize they're both tanned, only the colonel's hands have bigger knuckles and lots more lines. Like her face, her fingers look weathered, and her short brown hair seems windblown with a smattering of natural sun bleach, and frayed at the edges.

Dad joins the circle, and for a few minutes, it's just the five of us—Dad and the colonel and Ms. Franks and Chief Smith and me, sitting in the quiet living room with Captain Evans the not-witch who is probably older than she looks floating like a light-haired ghost at the left edge of my vision.

"You were going over what happened after school," Chief Smith prompts, and I tell him about the math test and the teacher Mr. Watson standing too close to Sunshine and making her nervous.

"He does that all the time," I say. "I've asked him not to. I've told my folks—pretty sure Sunshine's told hers, too, but he keeps doing it."

"I see." Chief Smith glances at Ms. Franks.

"It's his job," she murmurs without looking up at anyone. "He's supposed to challenge her."

Whatever. I wish he wouldn't do it. I keep telling Mom and Dad something's wrong with that guy, but no one listens.

Chief Smith makes his notes, and then I get to the part about going to the bus. "Roland Harks was there with his friend Linden Green."

"Harks and Green," Chief Smith says like he's talking with his teeth clamped shut. "Familiar with them."

"They're in our class, and Roland, he likes Sunshine but she doesn't like him, and he tried to bother us but Eli stopped him."

"Likes her?" Chief Smith glances at me, surprised and obviously not quite believing me, which irritates me because what, people can't be interested in Sunshine? Why? Because she rides a short bus?

Nobody believes what alphabets say. Not ever.

"Likes her," Chief Smith repeats. "As in . . . ?"

Everybody looks at me, Dad and the colonel and Ms. Franks and Chief Smith and even the ghosty-not-witch on the left, and the noise in my head gets louder because of all the eyes staring. I shift in my leather seat. Clear my throat. My face gets hot and so does my throat, and—

Talk, you idiot. If you don't say something, they're going to know. Know, know, know your boat, gently down the stream. What boat? Nobody's talking about boats.

—"Roland calls Sunshine *pretty girl*," I manage to say, then get double tense at the memory of that and how I wanted to hold her hand or hit him or do both and protect her and make sure Roland knew he couldn't have her—but I didn't.

Stupid idiot. Freak. Coward. Yellow, yellow, yellow, freak, freak, FREAK . . .

"He tries to get her to go out with him," I finish

lamely, all full of rage and shame and I know why but not really because it's too confusing, everything I feel about Sunshine especially when I don't feel much about anything else at all, thanks to my alphabet. "She doesn't want to. He won't stop sometimes, but Eli made him stop before we got on the bus."

Because I didn't.

Because I couldn't.

Freak, freak, freak, freak, freak, freak . . .

"Why didn't I know about this?" Ms. Franks asks, and she's staring at me now, which rattles me because she's Sunshine-Older-Model and she hardly ever stares at anybody. The question sounds like an accusation, or maybe that's just my alphabet, but the look on her face says that she thinks Roland liking Sunshine is some kind of crime.

"I—" I have no idea what to say, so the colonel says it for me.

"I'm sure the kids didn't think it was a big deal." She pats Ms. Franks's hand again. "Just daily stuff."

I nod and feel grateful to my mother. At least colonels in the army have a clue about which battles to fight when every day is a war. It doesn't do any good to try to talk about bullies, because nobody really hears us, and nobody can really do anything. They're alphabets, too, right? And alphabets like me, we might be confused. We might be making too much out of nothing. We might be a little . . . suspicious. Paranoid. Maybe we imagined the whole thing.

Chief Smith has been turning pages, and I realize he's writing names on the top of each one. I see *Eli* go by, and *Roland*, and as I finish my story, he adds *Linden Green*. After some hesitation, I see him write *Karl Franks* on the next page, and Dad's name on the one after that. When he's finished, he turns his attention to Dad.

"You were at work when this happened, right?"

Dad nods. "At work, then leaving for home. I follow the same schedule every day because of—"

He breaks off. Doesn't look at me. Doesn't say my name. "Because it's a good idea," he finally manages.

Chief Smith makes notes under Dad's name, then turns the page and I'm wondering why everybody got a page and whether or not I have a page and why that would matter, but Chief Smith keeps asking questions, like what time Mr. Franks was leaving to go out of town after Eli's appointment, and he makes some notes under *Eli* and *Mr. Franks*, and like an afterthought he makes pages for Ms. Franks and even the colonel but not the not-witch, and there's finally, finally a knock on the door and Dad goes to let in Drip and Drip's mom, and Chief Smith turns pages all the way back to the front of his notebook—and that's where my name is.

You're first. He thinks you did it. He thinks you took Sunshine, you idiot. You're in so much trouble. Trouble, trouble on the double. Nobody's in trouble. Everybody's in trouble.

My mouth gets dry, and it's hard to swallow but Drip

doesn't notice as he runs over all big huge eyes and his mouth open in a round O and drops down beside me, using the leather chair arm as a bench for his long, tall body.

"Find her yet? Anybody hear from her? Did she leave a note or something? Are people out looking?" His words flood the room, full of sound and feeling and everything I have inside and can't show because of my alphabet, but that's okay because Drip has enough feeling for every-body, even me.

Chief Smith gets up to make room for Ms. Taylor, who's long and tall like Drip and pretty like somebody on television, especially when she wears tailored pantsuits, which she nearly always does. Today, her outfit looks like brown silk, soft and no wrinkles anywhere, and she's got a bloodred scarf at the neck, and the color absorbs me because it's so bright.

Blood, blood, blood, freak, freak, freak, freak . . .

For a few seconds, as the colonel and Ms. Franks and Ms. Taylor talk to each other, there's no room in the universe for Drip and me and Dad and Chief Smith. We're as much on the edge as the silent not-witch who's just watching, and this, at least, seems normal. I don't care how much I read about men and women being the same. Sometimes they just aren't, and sometimes when women talk, there's no space for men or boys or anything that's not something they're choosing to include.

"Lisa, I can't believe she just didn't come home—"

"We'll find her, don't you worry—"

"Right here for you, honey, and we're not going *anywhere*—"

Lisa. It always surprises me to hear somebody call the colonel anything but Colonel—or Mom, which I haven't done in a long time, because . . . well, it's just hard for the colonel to feel like a mom most of the time. Lisa Jones Milwaukee. It's weird, remembering that colonels have first names. Derrick's mom has a first name, too. It's Denise, because his family tends to do *D* names, even where nicknames are concerned.

"You look in our place?" Drip asks me so quiet his voice barely gets through the voices of the women and the voices in my head.

"Not yet," I tell him, and then I feel stupid because I should have thought to go down by the river to our sitting spot.

Stupid, stupid, stupid, blood, blood, blood, freak, freak, freak . . .

It's hard not to imagine Drip's mom with her throat cut, because my brain does that to me sometimes, shows me awful things I'd never do and never want, like nightmares, only I'm awake. If I don't stop thinking about blood, I'll start seeing it, then everything will get one hundred times more awful.

I haven't looked anywhere for Sunshine. I just came

here with Dad. I'm as bad as the not-witch, just trotting along behind the people in uniforms. What's wrong with me? I haven't even gone to Sunshine's room.

She might be in there. Maybe she's just hiding under the bed or in the closet or she's really in the corner, pretending she's invisible so hard she's actually invisible and nobody can see her but me and—

Did you ever want to be invisible Sunshine asks and we're ten and everything's easy because it's summer and we're ten and we're in our sitting spot Sunshine and me and we're sitting and the sun glitters off her locket and Drip's splashing through the river and the world doesn't exist it's just us and I say yeah I've wanted to be invisible lots of times and she says close your eyes and I'll close mine and I do it because I always do what Sunshine wants and she laughs and she says we're invisible now at least until we open our eyes and then she sounds a little sad when she says maybe that'll be good enough and maybe it will be and I want it to be so she'll be happy like this every day all day and forever and

—Chief Smith is adding a name to his flip pages as Drip recounts the same day I told him about and I see Mr. Watson get a header.

Why?

Did Drip make him seem meaner than I did? Because Mr. Watson isn't mean. He's just pushy sometimes, especially with Sunshine, but Ms. Franks is probably right. That's his job.

"May I go to her room?" I ask, interrupting who-ever's talking and I don't even know who is, but every-body looks at me.

For some reason, I only want to look at Ms. Franks. "I just want to see—to be sure—"

My voice drops to nothing, just a chicken whisper, a silly rasp, but tears fill up her eyes and she says, "Of course you can."

Chief Smith says, "That's not a good idea. I don't want anything disturbed."

"I'll go with him to be sure he doesn't touch any-thing," the colonel says in her army voice, that hard don't-argue tone, and she's smiling, but it's not really a smile, and along the left-hand wall of the town house, the not-witch comes to attention.

"He needs this, I think," the colonel adds, and then Chief Smith looks embarrassed, and he apologizes, and he waves one hand toward Sunshine's room like, okay, if that's how to handle freaks, far be it for me to get in the way.

I don't look at Drip or Ms. Taylor as I launch myself out of the chair, and I'm away from the room and all the people and down the hall before anybody can decide dif-ferently.

Even before I get to her door, I smell it, the whispery scent of honeysuckle creeping around the apple smell of the place, gently moving it aside to make room for Sunshine.

The door's open, and there's a light on like she's in

there, and my heart pounds hard and then harder as I slow, then stop at the threshold and look inside.

Dark hardwood floors gleam beneath cream-colored throw rugs. Her bedspread is satin and green and thick, and I know it's soft. Her bed's full size, with a brass headboard, and her furniture—two dressers, one chest of drawers, a big mirror on a stand, a night table and a rocker, it's all a creamy old white with little flecks of color. Her phone's lying on her desk but her bag and books and notebooks aren't here and that's good because wherever she is she's got paper and pencils and pens to write poems with and she's got something to read even if it's just stupid school stuff.

My eyes travel to the bookshelves lining every spare inch of wall space, all stuffed with romance novels and fantasy novels and teen novels and literary *New York Times* stuff nobody I know but Sunshine reads. Everything is spotless like it got cleaned top to bottom just minutes before I showed up, and it's all motionless and empty like a photo because she's not here. I know without going in, without looking under the bed or in the closet or in the corner, I know Sunshine's not anywhere in the room, and this part may be like the movies because I know it because I don't feel her. I should feel her here, and I don't.

Let's go in here Jason because it's my space and I need it to be mine again I need to make it mine and right now it's private and that's important because I have to tell you something and she's got tears in her eyes and I want to lift my thumbs and wipe the tears away and when I do she lets me and then she's got her face against my chest crying and I hold her and I want her to stop stop stop crying but I don't know how to help her until she tells me what she wants and I still don't know how to do it but I'll try and I'll do my best because it's Sunshine and I'd do anything for her even give up all my own books and games and movies I'd do anything for her even die I'd do anything for her

I'm seeing black clouds. Spinning. Swirly. The clouds where last Saturday should be. Pain pokes at my temples and I stop because I have to stop trying to remember because I promised and once I promised so hard the clouds came and now I think it might put knives through my brain if I quit forgetting. Sometimes I don't know what I'm remembering instead of dreaming or dreaming instead of remembering but if I could make my dreams real, I'd dream Sunshine sitting on the edge of her bed, gazing up at me like everything's going to be okay. I'm in the room now, and I don't know how I got in here. The last thing I remember, I was at the door. Now I'm at the desk. I'm staring down at her phone. At the empty space beside the phone where a note should be: Dear Jason and Derrick and the colonel and everybody, I went to the mall— something. Anything but the blank white wood.

Can letters be invisible?

"Don't touch the desk, honey." The colonel's voice startles me enough to turn around, and she's standing in the door like I was a few seconds ago. She looks worried. Captain Evans is right behind her. The not-witch doesn't look worried, but her expression is intense and she's so on guard that if this were a battle game, I'd be pulling weapons and spinning in circles to see where the monsters are.

"She's not in here," I say, and I hate it but my voice sounds like a shaky baby-cry thing, and—

Stupid baby, stupid freak, row, row, row the freak, who's the freak, where's the freak, where's Sunshine, where's the freak, it's all your fault.

—The colonel's beside me the next second, like she blinked herself from the door into the room, and she gathers me up in her arms. She smells like the colonel, all leather and dirt and battle, but she feels like Mom as she holds me and tells me, "I'm sorry."

She doesn't say it's probably nothing, that it'll be okay, that we'll find her. The colonel isn't given to making promises she can't keep, and really, that's fine by me. I don't want to hear any of that right this second, because I wouldn't believe it and it wouldn't help.

Sunshine's not here. She's gone. She's really gone.

"That phone," Captain Evans says from behind us. "It's like she didn't want to be found—or someone didn't want us to be able to track her. I think it's time we call the FBI. It may not be an abduction, but they'll send a team if we put in a word."

"Do it," the colonel says, and she gets tense, fast and sudden, like she knows she's saying the right thing but worrying about it all at the same time.

Not-witch vanishes from the doorway, or maybe she just walks away. I can't tell. Time's skipping a little on me right now.

The colonel pulls back and stares into my face, into my eyes, like she's trying to find Sunshine hiding inside my forehead or maybe sneaking back and forth between my ears. "Do you need something extra to stay calm? Because I think that's very important right now."

Something extra. She means "PRN" pills. I used to think that stood for "per RN," as in a nurse gets to decide when a patient needs extra pills—because that's sure what it means in the hospital. I looked it up once, though. It stands for *pro re nata*, which is Latin for "as the circumstance arises." Freaks like me, people with alphabets, sometimes need PRN medication to keep our heads from exploding in stressful situations.

This would definitely be a stressful situation, but—

"No," I tell her. "I can't think if I take extra pills." Then, before she can argue, I add, "I need to be able to think for Sunshine."

The colonel gives this a second or two. She doesn't like it, but she nods, and people start talking louder out in the living room and I hear the not-witch explaining about how the FBI has a Child Abduction Rapid Deployment—CARD—with teams trained to find missing children, and how with a special request they might get involved right now.

"Don't push it with your inside agitation," the colonel tells me. She lets me go, still watching me like I might suddenly grab everything in the room and put my fingerprints all over it. "I know you hold it together well on the outside, but on the inside—if you start falling apart, tell me and I'll go to the house and get you something. And Jason, when the CARD team gets here, I want you to be careful what you say."

This makes me stare back at her like she might be the one about to fingerprint everything in Sunshine's room. "What do you mean?"

"I mean keep shut up unless they ask you questions, and when they do ask, answer—but don't go too far off track." The colonel frowns. She glances toward the living room, where everything's gone quiet, probably because the not-witch is phoning in the request for CARD to get involved.

"The FBI isn't like Chief Smith," the colonel says. "They might be fast-paced and pushy. They might be sharp with you and get you upset."

And she's worried about this—why? Her reputation? Dad's? Or for Sunshine's sake? It's hard to tell. I don't like the idea of talking to a bunch of pushy strangers, but—

But—

"Can they find Sunshine?" I ask the colonel.

She answers with an abrupt "Yes."

"Good enough," I tell her, and we leave Sunshine's room, which isn't as hard as I thought it would be, even though part of my heart stays behind.

THREE HOURS

The old dusty clocks on the old dusty walls of the VFW seem to tick louder than my own voices mumble. They're old-fashioned with hands and numbers instead of glowing digital lines and they all tell me how long Sunshine's been gone.

Three hours.

Tick-tick-tick-tick-tick. There's no *tock*. There's no alarm. It never stops. *Tick-tick-tick-tick*, and *swish-swish-swish-swish* as I sweep because I'm sweeping with an ancient broom, the kind with old jaggedy straws on the end because everything here is out of date. Everything here is old and stupid and it's been three hours and I'm sweeping for the FBI and the FBI never comes to towns like this. We're a speck on the map. We're a freckle on the speck, maybe that tiny crumb you dropped last week—we're nothing and nowhere.

The nearest anything to us is the military base, Fort Able with its famed 85th Airborne Division, twenty miles north. That's where the colonel works, and it's huge, covering the corners of three different states and hosting around thirty thousand soldiers plus their families and all the support staff it takes to feed, clothe, house, and train that many men and women. It's where most everybody works if they don't farm, slog in the paper mill, teach at the schools, or man the shops and stores.

The FBI probably never even heard of where we live until they got the call from some uppity-muck friend of the colonel's at Fort Able, pulling in favors and asking for help. The colonel tells us the team is already in the air and on the way. They'll have lodging at Fort Able, but we'll need to find a good hub of operations for them to set up their equipment. Chief Smith talked to local folks and veterans, and the largest building in town not counting the schools—the old brown brick-and-stone VFW hall on the hill—got the nod. It's close to the school and where we all live, and it's halfway between the police station and the fire station, overlooking the town like some run-down sentinel that can't keep us safe anymore. It's strong but it's old and it's dirty and I'm sweeping and three hours turns into four hours.

Four hours.

And four hours, that turns into five hours.

And the clocks keep ticking and I'm thinking I should go look in Sunshine's room or on the bus or all along where the bus drove or maybe at the school but the police have already done that and Sunshine's brother, Eli, has done that and they're probably doing it all over again so I can't help there and I can help here with the sweeping but it's been five hours, and it's more than five hours now.

With the half-moon hanging like a broken Christmas ornament in the night sky, Dad and Drip and Chief Smith and I finish sweeping the VFW. We've got the windows open to air everything out, and we've set up tables and chairs in all the rooms like the colonel ordered. There's the big main area where the VFW does dinners and stuff, a kitchen, two bathrooms (one for each gender), then twelve smaller rooms—offices, storage, empty—each one has a table and at least four chairs now. The whole place smells like Pine-Sol, and everything's too quiet because nobody's talking. From the other rooms off the main area, the scuff and clatter of shoes and brooms on brown tile and ancient concrete sounds like demented Morse code.

S-O-S.

When I was little, I thought that meant *Save Our Sh*— well, you know, because I heard the colonel say it once. The FBI is coming to do that, only it's *Save Our Sunshine.* I'm glad, but I'm also scared—not because I have anything to worry about, but because the colonel was scared. I could tell when she told me to watch what I say. The colonel gets freaked out by my crazy voices sometimes, but she'd protect me to her last drop of blood if anything came after me.

Why would she think she has to protect me from the FBI agents? If they're really coming here to find Sunshine, I'll do whatever I can to help them.

She thinks you did it because you're a freak. Idiot. I can't believe you're such an idiot. Fool on the hill, fool on the hill, fool on the hill. Did what? Did who? Did where?

I realize I'm standing in front of the closet in the main area, broom in my hand, frozen as I listen to the voices. I hate it when I do that.

"Maybe nobody did anything," I mutter back to the noises in my head. I hate it when I do that, too.

But Sunshine could have run away or gotten lost. Everybody's saying that and it might be true. Maybe nobody snatched her. Maybe nobody hurt her.

Somebody was hurting her. She told me that, didn't she? Last Saturday—

The swirly clouds clot across my eyes and pain jabs into both sides of my head. My fingers curl into fists, and there's a roar and it's all my voices at once and they're all saying *promised promised promised* but this is bad, it's an emergency and I need to know but I can't know because I promised and if I break a promise to her I'll die because that's what should happen.

Do I know something I should be telling people?

You're just a freak. You're just a stupid freak. Freaks don't speak. Freaks shouldn't speak. Don't talk out of your head or the swirly clouds will eat you because sometimes clouds have teeth.

I don't know for sure. *Keeping your mouth closed is rarely a bad idea*, according to another Dad-ism. I might be remembering alphabet voices and alphabet pictures and that's not something I need to tell Chief Smith or the FBI. Please don't let anybody be hurting Sunshine. Please don't let anybody hurt her ever. Does the colonel think something happened to Sunshine? Does she think I had something to do with it?

How could she think that?

"Because you're a freak," I say with my voices, and I really, *really* hate it when I do that.

The clouds go away and the pain in my head eases and I put my broom back in the closet. None of this feels real to me, and I can't believe it's dark and the stars and moon are out, glowing and twinkling through the dark-paned windows, but Sunshine isn't home. Her mom and Ms. Taylor are still at Sunshine's place, waiting for Mr. Franks to get home and hanging by the telephone because Chief Smith told them to stay there in case Sunshine tries to call or comes home. Drip's brothers are out driving the roads. Sunshine's brother, Eli, is walking the neighborhoods around Sunshine's town house again, even though the police have done it three times now. I can imagine his hands balled into fists, *PAIN* and *HOPE* flashing from his fingers with each step he takes.

Stupid, stupid ass. This is all your fault. You're a coward. Yellow, yellow, yellow. You're yellow. Everything's yellow.

The voices are so loud my fingers dig into the closet door. My regular pills are due, but if I send Dad for them or ask the colonel to go get them when she gets back with the FBI team, I'll go to sleep. There's no choice about that. Take fuzzy pills and zonk goes the Freak boy. I can't help find Sunshine if I'm in dreamland, so I'm waiting, and it's not that big of a deal. I can miss a day, or even two or three. The medicine stays in my blood a long time. Things get hard, but not too awful, at least when it's not stressful.

Drip comes charging into the main area carrying his broom. His movements are jerky and twitchy and way too clumsy and fast, and I know his meds have worn off, too. His meds aren't like mine—he takes anti-fuzzy pills to help him focus, but they're only good for part of the day. Toward bedtime, he burns out and gets wild, then all of a sudden—boom—just goes to sleep wherever he is, whatever he's doing.

"You think we should go to our spot?" Drip bangs into me as he tosses his broom into the closet and shuts the door. "I know it's dark, but we could get flashlights and she might be there. What if she's there?"

Drip's talking too fast just like he's moving too fast,

and he's sweating, and his eyes keep going left and right as his fingers twitch and jump. He can't help it. It's his alphabet, and the effects of his meds.

"Keep your voice down," I tell him, glancing at the double glass doors leading into the VFW hall like the FBI might be right outside listening. They aren't, but Chief Smith and Dad could hear him without a lot of trying.

Drip nods. His big round eyes study me.

"I don't have a flashlight," I tell him. Then I sigh. "Maybe we should tell Chief Smith and let him go with us—or send one of his officers."

"To *our* spot?" Drip doesn't like the idea. I can tell from the monumental frown. "If she's there, she'll be pissed and upset. That's our place, Freak. It's our secret place."

"It's a spot on the river. It's not exactly secret."

"But it's ours."

And what he means is, it's hers and she shared it with us and—

Promise you'll never show anybody else because this is where I come when I can't take people and faces and voices anymore she says and we're eleven the three of us and she's kept this secret for years about her place and it's quiet and beautiful and out of the way and we swear we won't tell anyone and we thank her because it's the perfect place for people like us and Drip goes in the water and she looks at me with those sad sad serious eyes and she holds her locket tight and she asks me do people ever get to be too much for you Jason and yes I tell her yes because they do they really do but I'm thinking that she won't ever be too much for me because she's as perfect as this place and she smiles and that just makes her more perfect and

—"We can't tell anybody," Drip mutters, but it doesn't matter because right that second the double glass doors swing open and the colonel marches in with Captain Evans and behind them come a bunch of soldiers in casual fatigues lugging boxes and folding tables and chairs and some video screens and bulletin boards and chalkboards and behind them come five more people, three women and two men. They have on rumpled-looking suits, all of them, and they fan out, pointing and directing the soldiers.

I feel like Drip and I are shrinking, becoming less and less a part of this world as the VFW hall starts to turn into something else, some other place, and I hear the colonel barking orders and Captain Evans saying, "No, not here, Private. Over there."

Then Chief Smith and Dad come into the main area and start shaking hands with people and introducing themselves, and the guy standing in the middle of the room seems to be in charge of the FBI team. I take him for around fifty years old. He's about six feet tall, in decent shape, and he's got short, buzzed gray hair like he might have been military a long time ago. When he thrusts out his hand to Dad and says, "Special Agent Robert Mercer," his voice is deep and authoritative.

After he and Chief Smith exchange names, Agent Mercer gets right to it with, "Sunshine Patton is seventeen years old, and as with any adolescent, it's possible that she left on her own, that she ran away. However, because of her mental illness, she's considered a vulnerable child, and we're treating this as a mysterious disappearance. You made a wise choice, involving us as quickly as possible. These first twenty-four hours are absolutely critical because after that, outcomes in situations like this aren't good. My people will help coordinate with your department and state resources, and we'll organize the investigation, searches, and technical aspects. If necessary, we'll consult with the Behavioral Analysis Unit."

"Don't they do serial killers?" Drip whispers, only it's not so much a whisper since his meds wore off and he's bouncing on the balls of his feet and swinging his arms back and forth even though he's sort of hiding behind me at the same time.

Special Agent Mercer's attention shifts to us, and for a long moment, he regards Drip. Then he focuses on me. Even from halfway across the room, I feel the ice of his merciless gray eyes. He's got this straight-line mouth that isn't made to smile, and—

He knows it's your fault. He knows you're an idiot. Fool on the hill. Fool on the hill. He's got cold eyes. Why does he have cold eyes? He's probably a serial killer.

—"We can also access resources at the National Center for the Analysis of Violent Crime Coordinators," Agent Mercer continues, never taking those chilly eyes off my face, "and Crimes Against Children investigators. All operations will run through this command post—and the first thing we'll do is set up a map of registered sex offenders in this area." He turns to Chief Smith. "Your officers can start with canvassing those individuals, and we'll call in state police if you don't have enough manpower."

He stops. I wonder if he's taking a breath. Do men like him have to breathe? At least he finally stopped looking at me. I think I need to go to the bathroom.

Chief Smith seems stunned. So does Dad. The colonel and Captain Evans have gone silent, but their squadron of privates keeps worker-beeing in every direction, setting up the . . . command post. Jeez. This seems more military than the colonel's job, and my stomach gets tight, then tighter and Chief Smith's stun passes over to me, and all I can think on top of the never-shutting-up voices is:

She's gone. Sunshine's really gone.

"Registered sex offenders," Chief Smith says, like it's finally all sinking in and his brain's starting to fire a few neurons. "What kind of radius are we talking about? Because we don't have too many of those folks around here."

"We'll do a thirty-mile grid to begin with," Agent Mercer says, frowning at a soldier who almost dropped a computer screen. "If that touches Fort Able, I trust that

Colonel Milwaukee will assist in gathering pertinent information and setting up interviews."

"Absolutely," comes the answer, but it's from Captain Evans, not the colonel. Weird. The colonel never lets anybody speak for her.

Dad notices this, too, because I see his eyebrows pinch and his eyes say, *Who is this woman?*

And I really need to go to the bathroom and I'm wondering, *Why is she here?*

Agent Mercer isn't finished. "We'll need to conduct our interviews as quickly as possible. Colonel Milwaukee tells me you've made an initial list of persons who might have key information, Chief Smith?"

Chief Smith stands motionless for a few long seconds, like he's still having trouble processing all the hustle and bustle and this man's firm, almost demanding tone, but then he clicks into gear and pulls his notebook out of his waistband. He holds it out to Agent Mercer, and the second the FBI man touches the paper, my heart thumps and pitches because it's *that* notebook, the one Chief Smith had at Sunshine's place, where he was writing down names and on his list, on the list of people to be interviewed, I remember what's first on that list.

My name.

The room's low fluorescent lighting suddenly seems too bright, and I swear I can hear the whine of the bulbs right through—

He's gonna know you're a lying, stupid little shit. You've got no hope. Give up now. Quit now. Give it up, give it up, give it up. Give up what? There's nothing to give up. Is there?

—"Oh man, oh man, oh man," Drip says over and over and over again in his not-really-a-whisper. "This is like a television show but it's real and where is she, Freak? Where is Sunshine?"

My own voices are bad enough. If I had duct tape, I'd keep Drip from adding to them, but I know he can't help it, and Agent Mercer is gathering two of his people, one man and one woman, and he's asking Chief Smith to get them to Sunshine's house to talk to Eli and her parents and Ms. Taylor.

Chief Smith gets on his cell, and a few seconds later, he says a deputy is on the way.

"I could take them to save time," Dad offers, but from across the room, the colonel shakes her head.

"No," she says, and it's her most-colonel-voice-ever tone.

I flinch at the sound. So does Dad.

"Oh man, oh man, oh man," says Drip, and—

You're so dead. You're stupid and YOU'RE DEAD and you might as well DIE NOW because you're first and this bastard's gonna grind you to dust. Dust in the wind. Dust in the wind. What wind? Who's talking about wind?

—I need to go to the bathroom. More than anything, I wish Sunshine were here. If she were here, I'd talk to

her and I'd stop being nervous because she could do that
for me and—

*I wish I could help you like you help me I tell her and I tell her
you always help me calm down you make everything better and
quieter and calmer and sometimes I think you're magic and she
says you can help me and we're back to that and she says you can
help me Jason and what am I supposed to say to her because I
never could say no to Sunshine and*

—Pain stabs at my head and my eyes water and Agent
Mercer's standing right in front of me, and his gray eyes
are even colder than I thought, and the lines at the corners don't soften them at all and I realize time skipped
and he's looking at me and I wonder if he said anything.
Did he ask me something? I'd look at Drip to find out,
but Drip's gone, bouncing across the VFW hall and wiping his nose and poking at all the computers and screens
getting set up, and Captain Evans is trying to keep him
from breaking anything. Dad and the colonel are standing a few feet away, watching me.

"Well?" Agent Mercer says, and I can tell from his
tone he's repeating himself.

"Sorry," I say, my face getting hot. "I didn't hear you."

His eyes get narrow like he doesn't believe that, but
he goes with it. "All right. Okay. Your mother warned
me you get distracted sometimes."

Idiot. Total fool. He's going to know. They always know, people like him. People, people, here's the church and here's the steeple. Steeples go on churches.

I don't cover my ears, which is a plus. "I do get distracted. But I'm listening now."

"It's my understanding that you have a close relationship with Sunshine Patton?"

Close relationship. Yeah. That covers a ton of ground. I think about my words for a few moments, and then I settle on: "She's my best friend. Sunshine and Drip and me, we've been in class together since we were little."

Special Agent Mercer raises Chief Smith's notebook. "You're the first name on the list."

"Okay." Deep breath. I'm ready. I need to do this. I want to do it, but before he can tell me where to go for him to talk to me, Captain Evans walks over to us, and the colonel's saying something to Dad, and Dad's pinching his eyebrows at her, then at Captain Evans.

Captain Evans beckons to my parents. The colonel comes toward us immediately, and Dad trails behind, one big pinch-face going on, but I don't have time to wonder about that.

"Are you going to cooperate with me, young man?" Agent Mercer's voice has dropped low, like he doesn't want my parents to hear him.

Even though it's hard for me to make out what he says

over the roar of my voices and the pounding of blood in my ears, I come back with "Yes, sir."

"It's not typical that my first interview is with the son of the people who called me to ask for my help with a case." Agent Mercer smiles, but it's even less of a smile than the colonel's when she's about to chew off your head at the neck, and I realize for some reason, he doesn't seem to like me, and I get the first glimmer of why when he adds, "It's definitely not typical to have a JAG lawyer on the spot."

My gaze jumps to Captain Evans. JAG? That's the Judge Advocate General staff—a lawyer? The colonel brought a *lawyer* with her?

Without skipping a heartbeat, Agent Mercer asks, "Do you think you need a lawyer, Jason?"

"Agent Mercer." Captain Evans has a head-chewing smile, too. "He doesn't understand things like this. Let's just get someplace quiet, and you can ask him whatever you need, so long as it's relevant to finding the girl."

She brought a lawyer. She knows. He knows. They all know. You're so stupid. You're such an idiot! Know, know, know your boat. You're crazy. Please stop talking about boats.

Everyone's here now, the colonel and Dad and Captain Evans and Agent Mercer, and I'm wanting to say, *You think I need representation? Why?* And I'm wanting to say, *I don't need a lawyer,* and I'm wanting to say, *Whatever, I'll do whatever, lawyer, no lawyer, whoever, whatever, if it'll help find Sunshine.*

I glance from face to face. I try to breathe. I try to hear my own thoughts scattered between the shouts bouncing across my skull and through my ears and falling out my eyes. What I say is, "I have to go to the bathroom."

That, at least, is the truth.

SIX HOURS

Twenty-four hours. That's not a long time. Two tens and a four. Simple math. And it's already been six hours. Twenty-four minus six is eighteen.

My gut seizes at the thought.

Eighteen hours *really* isn't a long time.

This isn't real.

I'm in a television show or a movie or a book and this isn't real and my best friend isn't missing and I'm not sitting with the colonel and Dad on my left and a JAG lawyer on my right, across a bare wooden table from an FBI guy with Chief Smith's notebook, frost eyes, a wicked crew cut—and something like a bad attitude, directed straight at me.

"When was the last time you saw Sunshine Patton, Jason?"

His voice sounds hard. Almost angry. What did I do to him? Is it because of the lawyer the colonel brought? Does he not like how I look? What?

He knows you're a freak. He knows you're stupid. Freaky freak freak. Maybe he's not mad. Maybe he is mad. Should he be mad?

The cinder-block walls make the room feel smaller and stuffier, but the lights are bright and I can see every tight line of Agent Mercer's not-so-nice face. The air still smells like pine cleanser and bleach and my eyes water a little bit only maybe it's not exactly water.

Crybaby. You're such a weak little snot. You should hate yourself. Hate, hate, hate, hate. Hate is a terrible word. Nobody should hate anything.

"I saw Sunshine when we got off the bus." Third time I've told him. He keeps asking the same stuff in different ways. I have no idea why, and no idea why he looks madder when my answers don't change. Maybe he doesn't look mad, but his face is melting, going empty in the center, or maybe that's just my brain. My eyes lie to me when I'm stressed.

Where is Sunshine?

Stressed is a good word for right now.

"Jason," Agent Mercer starts again with his melty face and his pissed-off eyes—

"Freak. Everybody calls me that. You can." The words fly out and saying that makes me feel better. It makes me feel normal and it makes his face stop melting. Sunshine's gone. How can anything be normal again? Maybe everybody's face should melt.

Agent Mercer's thick eyebrows lift. "Freak," he says, all surprised and slow. I can tell he doesn't want to look away from me, but his eyes travel straight to the JAG lawyer. "You want me to call you Freak," he says to me, but he's really saying it to her.

Why?

Freak, freak, freak, that's what you are, that's what I am, spam, ram, ham, ham, Freakity-freak, spam ham. I could use some bacon.

"We'd prefer you call him by his proper name," the lawyer says. I can see her reflection in the big glass window behind Agent Mercer, and she's doing the head-chew smile thing while the colonel frowns and Dad bites the inside of his left cheek. He does that when he's irritated. His eyes move side to side a little too fast, and that I haven't seen before. Something's bothering him, something more than all this, but I have no idea what it is.

"Why do people call you Freak, Jason?" Agent Mercer's using a you-must-be-brain-dead voice, pronouncing things too much like I'm hearing impaired instead of an alphabet.

"Because I'm nuts," I tell him, getting ticked, but the JAG lawyer puts her hand on mine. "I'm an alphabet. Alphabets are freaks. Everybody knows that."

"Alphabets," Agent Mercer repeats, obviously confused.

The colonel explains about the letters and labels, and then when Agent Mercer still seems confused, Dad adds, "It's a word Jason and Sunshine and Derrick use to describe themselves as a group. It feels better to them than any of the disorder-disability talk."

"Alphabets," Agent Mercer says again, like he's trying it out and maybe getting it a little and understanding—relating? Even if he doesn't want to. Then he starts over with, "So, why are you called Freak?"

"Stick to questions relevant to the girl," the lawyer warns Agent Mercer. She's still got her hand on mine, and when I try to move my fingers, she puts enough pressure on my wrist to keep me still.

Agent Mercer frowns and it makes him look sarcastic and nasty. "You don't think his nickname is relevant, Captain Evans?"

"I don't think it matters—" Dad starts, but the colonel jumps on top of him with, "I think law enforcement would be all too happy to focus on Jason as a suspect because he's mentally ill. What playground bullies choose to call Jason because of his disability is no concern of yours. He's here to help, Agent Mercer, not to volunteer as your primary person of interest."

Dad closes his mouth. Captain Evans closes her eyes. Opens them. She's still smiling, but more nervous now.

It's all a circus to me. I feel like a clown on the sidelines, with absolutely no clue what the main act is doing.

"Is that how we're playing this?" Agent Mercer asks, and I can't tell if he's talking to the colonel or Captain Evans but I don't care.

"I'm not playing," I tell him, jerking my hand away from Captain Evans. "I don't care if you consider me a Jason or a freak or a person of interest or disinterest or anything else. We've only got eighteen hours before twenty-four is up, and I want you to find Sunshine, so could you stop arguing with all of them and get to it?"

Agent Mercer's eyebrows lift again, but only for a second. The colonel and Captain Evans blink at me. Dad nods. I think he looks happy, but who can tell? The middle of his face is melty like everybody else's and I have to start looking at the wall because it creeps me out to keep my eyes on that weirdness.

"You say your last contact with her was after you got off the bus." Agent Mercer's voice makes an echo inside my head. "Right after school."

"Yes. I've told you that three times now. Can you get to the part about asking me questions that might help find her?"

A pause.

He's probably looking at my red face. At the way I'm making fists. Well, let him. This isn't helping Sunshine. We should be up and out of here and looking. Anything but this.

"Do you get frustrated easily?" Agent Mercer sounds happier now, like he's finally getting somewhere.

"No. I mean, I don't think so." I let out a breath and make myself look him in the eye, which is hard because his eyes seem wrong and square and melty but that's just my alphabet and I need to ignore it. "This is just—I want you to find Sunshine."

Agent Mercer looks even more happy. "Do you get angry easily?"

"No." In the reflection behind him, my own face starts to melt. I'm a painting, dissolving down the glass.

"Jason rarely gets angry at all," the colonel says.

"Everybody gets pissed. Isn't that right, Jason?" Agent Mercer smiles and I shiver, because in a melty face, that bunch of teeth seems demonic.

Focus.

How can you focus? You're an idiot. You don't know how to focus. Hocus pocus, hocus pocus. Magic has no place in this conversation.

Does this nutjob really think I'd get mad at Sunshine? He doesn't know anything. He can't know anything about me or her or our lives to ask that, because—

You can do it Jason I know you can I know it's scary but look at me yeah like that look right at me you know it's not real nothing's real but me and I'm right here breathe Jason you can do it you can think through what you hear and what you see it's not real but we are we are real Jason look at us look at me

73

—Skin stops sliding down faces and Dad looks like Dad and the colonel looks like the colonel and then there's Agent Mercer and the lawyer and I guess they look normal now, too. "I don't have a bad temper, if that's what you want to know," I tell Agent Mercer. "I don't throw fits or punches or go off and beat on walls or girlfriends. That's not my alphabet."

He doesn't believe me. I don't really care. But he smiles and asks, "Is Sunshine your friend or your girlfriend?"

See? Idiot. He knows. Everybody knows. You suck. Lots of things rhyme with suck. Should I make a list? Nobody needs lists. They've got enough lists and you're on them all.

My lips are moving and I'm trying to answer and—

I don't think it's a good idea but she says please and she's got tears and she says it'll make everything better that she knows it will and then she's in front of me and she's touching me and she's crying so what am I supposed to do even though I don't really know what to do but it's Sunshine and I have to make her stop crying because if she keeps crying I'll shatter inside and there won't be anything left of me and her locket presses into my chest and she feels like warm softness and she smells like warm softness when I hold her and

—And I'm seeing the clouds and the knives stab my brain and I turn it all loose and say, "I've never had a girlfriend."

Man, did that come out quiet. My face burns, but not

because I'm pissed or anything. I don't glance at the colonel or Dad before I start staring at the table, but I'm not sure why. They know I'm a loser.

"I find that hard to believe," Agent Mercer's saying.

I manage to look at him. "That's because you're not a freak."

"Jason." The colonel and the lawyer, both at the same time.

Then it's Dad's turn. "Let the boy talk, Lisa. It's how he feels—that's his truth. His truth can't hurt anything."

I'm trying to listen and trying to care, but is she my girlfriend? I mean, I want her to be, but is that what she wants, because I never know for sure. Should I put a name on it, some kind of label? She's just Sunshine, and that's plenty enough.

I wish I could go to Sunshine's room again. Maybe if I looked harder, I'd find a message. Maybe she wrote me a note and tucked it in one of the books she's always reading. Maybe she scratched something in the wood under her bed or left me a map like a treasure hunt in her pillowcase.

The colonel and Dad and the lawyer yammer at each other but I'm looking straight at Agent Mercer and he's looking straight at me when I ask, "Are you searching her room?"

Everybody shuts up like I spit on the table or something.

Agent Mercer's eyes narrow. "Why do you think we should do that?"

"Maybe she left something there to tell us where she went." I'm making fists again, but I can't help it. All this sitting and yammering, it's stupid and it's not helping anything. I thought this man came here to find Sunshine. Guess I'll have to do that myself.

"You think she went on her own—that she ran away?" That question came from the lawyer and I can tell Agent Mercer doesn't like her butting in to his inquisition.

"I don't know," I tell her, glad somebody's asking better questions. Better questions might make me think and if I think maybe I can get past all the noise in my head and find the right answers.

Would Sunshine run away? She had tons of reasons.

Yeah, you're one of them, you piss-poor excuse for a human being. Be, be, be, see, see, see, see-saw, back and forth and up and down. Maybe you're not a human being. Maybe not.

"I guess maybe I'm hoping she did run away," I say, "because if she ran away, she might have left us a note."

"And if she left you a note," Agent Mercer says, "it would be in her room?"

"Yeah. Because we weren't at school, so it couldn't be in her locker, unless she planned stuff for a long time and left the note before we went home. There might be a note, right?"

That sounded desperate. Sadness spreads across everybody's face except Agent Mercer's, because I don't think he's a sadness kind of guy.

But if there was a note, it wouldn't be in her locker or

her room, would it? Sunshine would never leave words for other people to find. The only place she'd leave anything like that is where only I would find it, or maybe Drip, because she knows Drip would give it to me.

I have to work not to go statue stiff and turn red as a strawberry.

Drip was totally right earlier. Why didn't I listen to him?

I don't need to be here listening to this man's stupid questions. Sunshine's been gone almost six hours. Six hours out of the twenty-four the FBI says she's got before . . . before things get . . .

Eighteen hours left.

Drip and I need to go down to the river, to our spot, to our place—to Sunshine's place—because whatever she left us, if she left us anything, it'll be somewhere by the quiet, cool running water.

And it'll be private.

Sunshine wouldn't want anybody to have her words but us, least of all this jerkoff of an FBI agent who isn't really trying to find her.

We need to get a flashlight and sneak out of here.

"Are we done?" I stand, already wondering how long it'll take Agent Mercer to ask Drip the same questions twenty times. Maybe other agents are interviewing Drip. Maybe they're already done. If they're finished, he and I can—

But—

Everybody's looking at me. Agent Mercer, the colonel, Dad, and the JAG lawyer. Nobody seems very happy, except maybe Agent Mercer.

I don't get mad much, but I'm mad now.

"Do you have somewhere else to be, Jason?" he asks, nasty-nice, and that's it. Really. Had enough of him.

"Yes," I tell him. "Outside finding my best friend."

Feeling hot, feeling cold, wanting out before stuff starts melting again.

I turn before he can say anything else. The colonel's calling my name and Dad's telling her to stop and the JAG lawyer's saying something to Agent Mercer and when I open the door and step into the hallway—Roland Harks is right there, right in my face with his serial killer eyes and his black hair and that smirk and he's melting and the way he looks and the way he talks and why didn't I think about him before? Why was I the one getting hammered when this monster was five feet away on the other side of the door?

"What's with you?" he mutters.

I grab the front of his black rock band T-shirt with both hands and yank him right into my own face.

"What did you do to her?"

"Hey!" Somebody's yelling. A woman. "You—what— let him go!"

She's right beside us like she slipped out of the shimmery melty air and she's older, maybe a mom or a sister or an aunt but my brain pushes that away because it's not natural for vermin to have family members.

"Where is Sunshine?" I grip Roland's shirt twice as tight and he grabs my wrists, frowning, pushing at my hands and he's gonna go off and smack me and for once I don't care, for once I'll smack him back because there's no Sunshine to protect and no Sunshine to get upset and maybe Roland and his pretty-girl this and get-a-burger-with-me-pretty-girl that had something to do with it.

"Did you hurt her?" I shake him and he sort of lets me but he's prying my fingers off him and it throbs but I hold on anyway. "She didn't want a hamburger. She didn't want a hamburger with you!"

"Dude." Roland's shoving at me harder, playing nice probably because of the woman yelling for help beside him but his eyes are furious. His eyes say I'm going to pay. And then his eyes melt and his face melts and I let him go, and Dad's got me, and he's hugging me from behind and he's saying, "Breathe, Jason. Come on. Just breathe."

And from somewhere the colonel's saying, "He's upset, Mrs. Harks. I'm sorry."

And the lawyer's telling Agent Mercer, "You stressed him on purpose. This is exactly what we were trying to avoid."

And I can't see him but Agent Mercer's looking at me because I can feel his melting eyes on the back of my melting neck and I can almost hear him asking about my bad temper and asking if Sunshine made me mad and if I went after her like I just went after Roland and that woman's holding on to Roland, looking relieved and he's not paying me any attention even though I keep telling him, "She didn't want a hamburger. She didn't want a hamburger from *you*!"

We're moving, Dad and me, and he's taking me away from the questioning room and Agent Mercer and the hallway and Roland and even the colonel and the lawyer.

"I'm breathing," I tell him when I finally stop yelling. "Sorry. I'm breathing."

Dad's moving me forward, side by side, his arm around my shoulders, and Drip and his mom are standing way across the room by the front door. Drip's fidgeting and hopping around. He's moving back and forth. He's hyper but . . . kind of not, too. Like he's putting on a little.

I slow. Then I stop walking and Dad lets me go.

"That was a little tense back there," Dad says, and I nod even though I'm only part hearing him because Drip's staring at me now.

He lifts his eyebrows like, *What the heck?*

I lift mine.

He shows me his right hand.

He's got a flashlight.

SEVEN HOURS

For a few seconds, it seems like Drip and I are alone in the universe. The wide, clean hall of the VFW seems empty, and he's looking at me, and I'm looking at him, and we both know we're blowing out of here first chance we get.

It'll never work. Even you aren't that stupid. Idiot. Fool on the hill. Fool on the hill. I don't think idiot's a nice word. Maybe it's right, though?

Six hours. Almost seven.

Get it together, you freak.

That was my voice, not the voices. Well, you know what I mean.

Gradually the world starts to focus again and I see tables and computers and FBI agents and behind me I hear the colonel fussing with Dad and Dad dropping a

Dad-ism about stirring in muck making everything mucky and the lawyer arguing with Agent Mercer about questions and suspicions and for some reason hamburgers and from somewhere else, Roland's whining to his mother about how crazy I am. Drip's mom heads over to plow into some of them or maybe all of them because now's not the time for fighting and Drip's mom is big on only fighting at the right times.

Drip bounces up to me, still faking hyper. When he's close enough for only me to hear him, he says, "I took my medicine again. I'll be good for a few hours."

"Yeah, and awake until tomorrow?"

He shrugs. "That's a good thing, right?"

"I didn't take mine." I breathe like Dad wanted and wait for Drip's response, but I don't worry about him flipping out. Drip and Sunshine and me, we don't flip out on each other, no matter what. It's a rule.

He gives me a half stink-eye, though. "You got a few days before you go totally nuts, right?"

"A few."

We both know it'll get hard. That stuff in my head will come crashing apart—but usually I can hold it together for a while.

Usually.

Drip gives me another shrug. Then, "We going out the front door or the bathroom window?"

And the VFW people and space seem that much

farther away, and I dig through my memories of helping clean the place. "*Is* there a bathroom window?"

Third shrug. "Front door, then."

Seems reasonable to me. Everybody's too busy hollering at each other to care much what Drip and I do, so with one last glance at the arguing, typing, ignoring-us room, we walk right out the main entrance to the VFW.

A few running steps later, I realize one very important thing.

It's dark.

I mean, it's always dark at night, but some nights don't have any stars or any moon and glowy metallic clouds seem to snake toward the ground and there's fog and cool air and that's tonight. Dark. Dark and cold. Maybe because it was so bright and warm, almost hot, in the VFW behind us.

Drip leads because he's got a better sense of direction than I do, and because he's got the flashlight. I keep tripping over my own feet because I can't see where I'm going, but I can see Drip's shoulders so I keep my eyes locked there and follow.

"Did you get questioned?" I ask him.

"Yeah, but it was stupid. I think the guy asked me ten times what time we left. Why do they ask everything ten times?"

"I don't know." But I feel better. At least I wasn't the only one that got treated like nobody believed him.

"It kinda pissed me off," Drip says. "Why are they wasting time? That main guy said we've got twenty-four hours to find her, that this first twenty-four is so important, so they waste it jawing at us?" Every step we take, he talks faster and louder. "They don't have a clue, but maybe we do. Do you think she's there, Freak? Man, will her folks be pissed. Maybe she fell asleep. Do you think she fell asleep?"

"She didn't fall asleep." Now I wish he'd stop because his questions make my heart hurt. His questions make me know it's not really likely Sunshine's at our place, but I want to hope she's there. Even if she's there, she'd never be asleep. If she's at our place, she's there on purpose, and she's hiding. Lots of things scare Sunshine. Some of them should.

Like you, you freak. Why did you do it? Why did you touch her? I wanna hold your hand. Hold your hand. Touching isn't wrong. She asked for it. But maybe Sunshine thought it was wrong?

Stop. Can't think about that right now. It's so dark, and it's getting colder, and the air smells like rain or maybe tears.

We wind away from the VFW down short blocks, then turn into a wooded area attached to the town's only park. To get to our place, we have to go through the park, down a hill, turn right, and follow the path until trees break on either side of us. The park's empty and the hill's empty, at least I think it is because I can't see anything other than the gray outline of Drip's back.

In the daytime the clearing we have to cross seems warm and pretty, but tonight it's not warm or pretty and when we run to the center of the open space in the woods, there's nothing but scary dark trees and they're everywhere, all around us, black marks against the black sky. My breathing's hard and my throat feels tight and the trees look like monsters reaching and reaching toward nothing because—

You're nothing. You're nothing. You're nothing at all and you're stupid and a big baby. Babies cry, babies sigh. Babies fly. Maybe the trees really are monsters?

—Drip's talking as we push forward but I can't hear him. I can't hear anything but static from the monster-trees and it makes my guts hurt and I want to scream but if I start screaming Drip will stop running and he'll probably have to drag me back to the VFW and I'll still be screaming and then I'll be in the hospital and—

It's not real Sunshine says like she always says when I get drowned by my own stupid not really real thoughts but sometimes they seem so real but she says no no Jason it's not real and we're here and everything's fine and that's why she can say to me we're here we're here please make it fine Jason please promise me you won't think about him or talk about him and I won't and we won't and we'll make him not exist please please we'll make everything okay again

and she presses her locket into my hand and she makes me squeeze
it and

—I stumble over a biting strand of blackberry bush and
smack into Drip from behind. He lurches forward with a
big loud "Ow!" Then "Be careful." Then we're out of the
scary clearing and the scary trees might be following us and
he asks, "Do you think she left on purpose?"

Yes.

No.

How close are we to our place?

"I don't know," I say to Drip, not really sure if I'm
answering my own question or his.

Our place—there's another turn, right again, and skirt-
ing along the bottom edge of a hill tangled with thorny
blackberry bushes. Where are we? It's so dark.

It'll always be dark without her . . .

On the path, that's where, I can tell because we've
worn it down through the rocks and sticks and underbrush, and here the thorns aren't so bad because we've
made a small opening in the bushes we keep clipped with
a pair of rusty gardening shears we hide in the dirt beside
the opening.

On the other side of the opening, that's our quiet place,
our special spot. The river moves fast alongside it, rushing
across a stone bed, all clear with white foam. There's nothing but trees on the other bank, and they aren't scary, and

the thorny bushes and hillside behind us, not scary. There's a big huge rock that hangs out across the river. A little bit scary, but not when we sit on it together talking about rivers and waters and the world or nothing at all. If it's raining, we sit under the rock, up against the part not in the river, and it's like a giant granite canopy above us, almost a cave, but not quite, and not scary. Not scary like the trees that aren't following us. Probably.

If I look back I'll fall.

"What if somebody grabbed her?" Drip's getting louder. "We have to find her. We have to know for sure, because if she needs help, I'm gonna help her. We're gonna help her, right, Freak?"

"Right." If she wants me to. Maybe she doesn't even want to look at me.

You know she doesn't. You're foul. You're filthy and awful and she knows that now. She'll never look at you again. No one looks, no one looks, no one looks. Maybe everybody is staring at you.

Drip slows all of a sudden and I bash into him again and we stagger forward together, out of the sticky bushes through the darkness breathing the cold black breathing the cold nothing and we both stop talking because we hear it then, the way the river does its own talking in our place. If it had a voice, it might say:

She was here . . .

She was here, but . . .

She was here but she's . . .

And my throat gets so tight I can hardly breathe and my chest burns and I need her to be here, I really, really need her to be here, please, please, please let her be here. I strain my eyes for any glimmer, any shadow, any movement. I pray for a whiff of honeysuckle, a whisper of skin or hair or sighs, the glitter of locket gold, just the tiniest trace. Anything. I'll take anything at all.

Drip sweeps the flashlight back and forth, back and forth and all around, and I'm breathing hard and my ankles smart from blackberry stings. When the light passes in front of me, I see the white-steel puff of my own breath.

"Sunshine?" he calls out, his voice too high and tight, and I say her name, too, calm as I can even though I really want to yell it or scream it or fall down and cry and start begging.

"Sunshine?"

And we stop, and we listen, and Drip swings the flashlight everywhere, too fast and not fast enough, and there's nothing but the big rock and the river and the distant trees and bushes behind us, there's nothing here but us, but there has to be something, she has to be here, I need her to be here.

Drip aims the light right at the shallow cave under the big rock, but nothing's there.

"Sunshine!" My voice shakes and I've got both fists clenched.

Drip whips the light to the left and I can't take it any-more so I grab the flashlight away from him, and he doesn't even fight with me, just keeps calling her, only he's more talking the name now, then whispering it in between when I yell it, then he says, "She's not here. I don't think she's here, Freak."

I don't want to stop. I poke the light left, then right. Then here, then there. Each time I slice the darkness I feel stupid hope, then stupider agony. "Don't say that. We haven't looked everywhere yet."

"She wouldn't still be asleep with all this yelling, and you know she's not hiding from us."

That's what he thinks. She might be hiding from you. She should be hiding from you because you're a freak and you stink. Freak stink, stink freak. Maybe everyone should hide from you.

"Right?" Drip's asking me and when I shine the light in his face his eyes look huge and wide and I don't know why but I just want to hit him. But really I don't think I want to hit him, I think I want to hit something because Sunshine's not here.

I knew better, but I wanted it to be true.

There's no moon and no stars and the weird glowing clouds drift lower, lower, like they're coming to crush us all. I glance at them, think about telling them to stop, then realize I'm getting the double stink-eye from Drip as he puts his hand up to shade off some of the flashlight glare. "Ease up with that."

Every now and then I make him nervous. Now is one of those times. I can tell. It's okay because I owe him a few of those, but it's not okay. I don't need to make him nervous now, because he's sad and upset just like me. I lower the light, and I don't say anything to the clouds.

"She's not here," I mumble, my lips feeling thick and achy like I ate blackberry thorns instead of stabbing them into my ankles running here. It smells like river and rain here. River and rain and black, black night—but it doesn't smell like Sunshine. "She's just not here."

"We'll come back in the daylight," Drip says in a slow way, like he's stinging from his own thorns. "We'll look better."

Hope blasts through me again, but I stuff it straight back down because I know better, I really do and I don't want to eat any more thorns. "Why? She's not here."

"She could have hidden something." Drip sounds stubborn. He's thinking about a note, too. And I realize both of us think it's possible she might have gone away on her own, and I wonder what Drip knows, and I realize neither of us wants to believe Sunshine would leave us with no good-bye. She wouldn't have. I don't think she would have. But maybe she would.

I hate it when I sound like my alphabet voices.

I hate it when I smear together like a wet photograph and get all sticky and can't tell the crazy voices from my own voice and what I'm seeing now from what I saw before and what I want to see now and what I wanted to see before and—

I know it might be hard later but I don't care anymore I can't care right now Jason I just need you I just need to feel I need to feel something better than this and I need it all to be over and I need it all to be okay you'll help me I know you will because you've always loved me and I've always

—The black clouds bite into my brain and my head snaps back and the words die and—

"Somebody's coming." Drip's voice blows a giant hole in what's left of my thoughts.

My hand tightens on the flashlight and I want to hit him all over again because did she really say those things or did I just want her to say them? Did I make it all up? Did I find excuses to do what I wanted? Did I want to do something?

At the edge of the world, those horrible clouds with the horrible pain inside them try to gather again and I know I have to stop trying to think about it but I don't want to, I need to think about it and remember for her and for me but it'll kill me and I'll die before I know and how will that help anything?

"Jason?" Faraway voices. "Jason! Derrick?"

Men. Women. Probably parents. Who knows. Maybe officers and FBI agents, too. Is it illegal to come to special places and think about whacking one of your best friends with a flashlight? Why can't they let me think? Why won't anybody let me think?

Drip's waiting and I get it all of a sudden. I have the flashlight. It's up to me to get us out of here before the faraway voices—the ones outside my head—catch up to us.

This is our place. No one else can have it—but everyone will if I don't move. Crap. Oh man. I shine the light around. Then I start running.

"Wrong way!" Drip yells, but I realize this as I splash into the river, then turn and charge back toward him, past the side of the big rock and past him, too, and then we're both running, out of our place, back to the path, the hill, the blackberry bushes and their thorns. Have to push it. Sticks bash my ankles and the thorns stab. They cut.

You deserve it.

I have to breathe.

You deserve pain because you're an ass and an idiot and this is all your fault. Thorns will cut you to ribbons. Thorns and knives and all the cops and agents and officers will slice you to pieces. Ribbon on the wind, wind on ribbons. Did Sunshine ever wear ribbons in her hair?

My ankles burn from the thorns. My fingers burn where I'm gripping the flashlight so tight. We're beside rock and hill and grass. Then we're not. The light bounces like crazy. My breath flashes out in gray puffs I barely see.

This isn't right. My heart, my chest—tight. Did I turn left or right? Drip's not stopping me. He might not care, as long as we're away from our place. More bushes. Then the trees. The awful, black, live-looking reaching trees. Clearing. We're in the clearing. I stumble to a stop and Drip grabs my arms from behind to keep from running right over me. I fumble the flashlight, but he grabs it and shines it straight ahead.

"Don't stop here," he whispers, words ragged against my ear. "This is too close. Keep—"

"Jason?" The colonel's voice. Some distance.

"Derrick?" That's Drip's mom. She's a ways off, too.

"Boys."

Drip and I both freeze in place.

That voice comes from right in front of us. It's not as familiar, but I know it anyway, even if I don't want to.

Drip says something under his breath, and I'm pretty sure he knows who it is, too.

He turns me loose and raises the flashlight.

About ten feet in front of us, Agent Mercer's standing in the clearing, staring straight over the yellow beam into our faces. Into our eyes. Pitch-dark or not, he's studying everything about us. I know he's trying to stop us and keep us here. He wants to hold us and read us. He folds his arms, and he doesn't look angry or worried or any of the emotions I hear coming from the voices of our parents.

Too far away. They might as well be in Egypt.

He should call out for them, to tell them that he's found us.

He doesn't.

But then, I knew he wouldn't, didn't I?

I can't see the future, but sometimes it seems like I can.

My heart's beating so fast I can't even hear the voices in my head, but I can hear Drip muttering something about going out, getting a walk, getting air, getting away, and I want to tell him to shut up, but why? He can say whatever he wants. We haven't done anything.

Yes, you have.

We haven't done anything and we can go out for a walk and besides this guy's not doing crap to find Sunshine and it's been hours, too many hours and we're losing seconds and minutes right now.

I suddenly wish I could hit *him* with the flashlight and I probably would except I'd have to snatch the light from Drip and he probably wouldn't let me.

"What do you want?" I ask instead, my words as hard as the punch I want to throw.

Drip jumps at the sound of me talking to an FBI agent like that—talking to anybody like that.

Agent Mercer's eyebrows lift like I managed to startle him, but his expression buttons down so fast I wonder if I imagined the flicker of surprise. He goes on staring at me like the flashlight hasn't blinded him and in the weird half-dark but too-bright light he doesn't look completely human and I wonder who he really is and what he really is and my heart beats even faster and—

"I want the truth, Jason."

Jason.

Not Derrick, or Jason and Derrick. He's talking just to me.

What does he know? How does he know anything? There's nothing to know, but maybe there is? Don't hit him. Can't hit him. But I *want* to.

Hit him. Hit him hard. He wants to hurt you. He wants to take you to jail and beat your face in. He wants you dead. Dead rhymes with red. Dead's a sad place to be.

"I told you the truth," I tell Agent Mercer but it's hard because I'm talking through my alphabet voices and my teeth at the same time.

The calling people and the dark night and even Drip's frantic breathing poof out of my awareness and everything breaks into spooky silence. Agent Mercer's a wraith in the harsh flashlight, he's a ghost, a bad wizard, a dream monster, but he's too solid and he's not moving he's not budging and I can tell he's the kind of man who never budges and never will.

"I told you the truth," I say again, but the wraith ghost wizard monster who won't budge shakes his head. Slow. Back and forth, just once.

No.

I don't believe you, Jason. I know you're lying, Jason. Liar,

liar, pants on fire. One day you'll have to stop lying even if you're a freak.

Agent Mercer's next words fly out solid and real as his scary body, straight at me like fists and scarier than the trees reaching through the night to grab him to grab me to grab Drip and everyone and kill us before we can take another breath.

"You're hiding something."

EIGHT HOURS

"Are you trying to scare him?" Drip's voice shakes but somehow he sounds strong in the flashlight-broken darkness of the clearing.

"Jason?" I hear in the distance, getting farther away. Dad. Leaving me. *Come back, Dad. We're here. We're right over here.*

"No," Agent Mercer says. "I'm not trying to scare anybody."

Liar. My voice? Alphabet voice? Can't tell.

Drip gives a big snort. "Well, you are."

"Why would you be scared of me?" Agent Mercer asks, and I hate how he does that, try to turn everything into—I don't know, some sort of proof that we're bad or awful or sneaky or whatever.

You are. You know you are. A filthy little sneak. Awful is as awful does and awful does, does, does. Shame on you for being sneaky.

Breathe. Gotta breathe. Can't lose it here in the dark, here in the woods where Sunshine should have been but wasn't. Focus.

Yeah. That's so easy.

"Freak gets scared of a lot of stuff," Drip's saying. "So do I."

Agent Mercer's expression, yellowy and strange under the flashlight, changes for a split second, then goes back to blank. His voice sounds just as blank when he says, "I thought your problems were with attention, Derrick. Impulse control. I didn't read anything in your school or medical files about fears or anxiety."

Drip's mouth comes open just like mine. How did he get those files? Much less read them on such short notice? And if he can do all that, why wouldn't he have a clue about why he scares us?

"My—you—" Drip shakes his head and appears to get hold of himself. He lowers the beam of the flashlight so it's on Mercer's chin. "You just read about me on a computer or paper or whatever?"

"Derrick?" So far away it's like a whisper. Drip's mom is leaving us, too, and I don't hear the colonel or the lawyer or anybody. They're all going the other way and this jerk, he keeps not saying anything to them and I'm not sure why I'm not yelling out for our parents and other people, except I sort of want a chance to talk to Mercer, to get him off my back, to make him see the truth and start trying—really trying—to find Sunshine.

"You don't know what it's like to have an alphabet," Drip adds to Mercer, sort of angry. "You don't understand anything about my problems, or about Freak's. Nobody listens to us. Nobody believes us. Nobody cares about what we think about anything."

That flicker crosses Mercer's face again. I can tell, even though I can see mostly his mouth, not the rest of him. Is he surprised? Pissed off? Who knows.

He's evil. He wants to arrest you. Maybe he wants to kill you. Death is peaceful. Death is quiet. You've read lots of poems about death.

My heart won't stop with the racing and it's hard to breathe and my ankles still sting from thorns. I try to focus on the pain to keep my mind sharp but the darkness, it's growing hands and fangs and it's hard not to stare at them everywhere the flashlight isn't.

Mercer's mouth shifts again at the corners—something to nothing—something to blank—as he studies us and doesn't notice the dark hands or dark fangs or how the darkness, it's getting meaner. For a few weird seconds, I could swear he's about to apologize. He doesn't say he's sorry, though. What he says is, "You're right, Derrick. I probably don't understand much about what either of you goes through every day."

"So stop scaring us." Drip sniffs, and even though the

dark's mean and getting meaner, I'm impressed because he's not usually so tough. Is he doing it for me? For Sunshine? She's worth it. I'm not so sure about me.

"I don't want to be scary," Mercer says. "I just want the truth."

Drip's not through being tough because he comes right back with, "You've got the truth—or all of it we know. What good does it do to ask us the same questions over and over? We should look for her."

"Is that what you were doing?" Mercer's so smooth he could be made of silk. Wonder if he'd be so smooth if he knew the night could bite him. Do darkness fangs have a name? Nangs, maybe. What about Farkness Biters? If I designed video games, I'd put in Farkness Biters and maybe I'd name the night hands, too, something like—

Don't give in to it Jason I know it's all scary the stuff you hear the stuff you see but it's not real look at me here squeeze my locket and look into my eyes and I do and her eyes they're like midnight with candles in the center all warm and soft and right and she's not scary because Sunshine's never scary except one day she will be only I don't know it and I don't want to know it and

—"Yes."

That was Drip. I suck in black night air. What if it's poison? But that's stupid. It's not poison. What was he saying yes about?

My right palm tingles in the center like I'm actually squeezing Sunshine's locket, her magic locket that makes her not afraid and turns my voices into whispers and makes my eyes tell me the truth, at least for a little while. I can almost feel the gold, warmed by her skin, hot against my hand—but—

But—

Focus.

I reach back, dig through my thoughts, try to skip past pictures of Sunshine and fangs and stuff and—oh yeah. Mercer asked if we were looking for her. Yes. That much is the truth. Good job, Drip.

Mercer's next question comes out slower and softer. "Did you expect to find her?"

No. But I was hoping. Does that count? I don't say anything out loud.

Drip covers us both with, "We were thinking maybe she got upset and she was hiding. She might only come out for her mom or for us, so we thought—it seemed like we should look for her."

He lifts the beam of the flashlight, catching Mercer full in the face again, and this time the man blinks and some spell comes off me.

"We needed to get out of the VFW and do something to find her," I say, but my voice sounds weird to me, like I'm somebody else, like I'm talking from a room in some house miles away. Maybe the spell didn't come off after all. "Something real. Something more than you're doing. We know her better than you."

Drip glances in my direction, one eyebrow up. I must have sounded weird to him, too. Maybe the air really is poison and it's making my throat die. If my throat dies, can I keep living? If Sunshine dies, can anything keep living?

She can't be dead. My chest goes tight and hurts like something's punching me. Maybe the dark. Maybe the trees. Maybe the Farkness Biters. I can't breathe. I want to cry but I can't cry because I'm too old and because we have to look for Sunshine. She has to be alive. I can't think about anything else. She's alive. She's alive.

Mercer's gaze stays steady and it's on me, I know it is, even if Drip's shining the light on his neck now. "What is it I'm not listening to right now, Jason—or what is it you're not sharing?"

"Nothing." *Nothing you need to know. Nothing that's any of your business.*

Why is Drip looking at me like that? Like Mercer. Like I've done something?

Because you have.

Drip needs to stop. Mercer needs to stop.

But Mercer doesn't stop. "If something happened, if something went bad, you can tell me. We'll work it out."

Short breaths. Pounding heart. I think I'm sweating in the cold. I know I'm making fists and hearing buzzy whispers and that's bad. "You think I did something to her. You think I hurt Sunshine."

I'm talking to Mercer but maybe I'm talking to Drip, too, but that's stupid because Drip would never think something like that. Would he?

"I think it's possible," Mercer says, and for a second, I'm not sure what he's talking about, but then I remember what I said.

And my heartbeat comes back. And my breath. Because there, he just admitted it, didn't he? That he thinks I hurt Sunshine. He thinks Sunshine is gone because of me.

You know he's right. You know you're scum. It's all your fault. All your fault. Faults make somersaults. Acrobats make somersaults. Why is it so cold out here?

Mercer thinks I hurt her and Drip probably thinks I hurt her but Drip's saying—no—yelling—at Agent Mercer.

"Dude! You're more nuts than we are. You don't know anything." Drip's laugh comes out like mean-dog barks in the dark woods and the flashlight beam bounces each time. "I thought you were supposed to be some kind of expert."

Before I can count to two, Mercer pops back with, "Do you have a temper, Derrick?"

And that's about all I can take. My turn to yell. "So, what? If one crazy kid didn't hurt Sunshine, it must be the other one? No wonder my mother got a lawyer before you ever showed up."

"Why *did* she bring a lawyer, Jason?"

Could have predicted that question, couldn't I? Of

course I could. And he follows up with, "Why does every-one call you Freak?"

"Because I hear voices!" Yelling feels good. The gray clouds puffing around my head feel good because they chase back the darkness and make me safer. "I think funny. I say stupid crap when my brain plays tricks on me. All of that makes me a freak. It makes me *Freak*."

"And my nose runs and my mouth runs, and that makes me Drip," Drip says. Then his volume drops. "Sun-shine never calls him Freak, just like she never calls me Drip. You know that, right?"

This time Mercer's expression does change, and it shows just enough sadness that my thoughts brake and swerve before speeding straight into fantasies of murder-ing him.

"Sunshine was different," he says, and I don't think he's poking at us or trying to get more information. Just stating what he's been told, what he's trying to understand.

"Yes," Drip whispers, right at the same second I do. "She *is* different."

Mercer nods. "Sunshine was special."

"Yes," we both answer, and I say, "She *is* special."

Was, were—I don't want him talking about Sunshine in the past tense any more than Drip does. It's wrong. She's not a was or a were or a used to be. Sunshine's an *is*, and I'll fight him over that if he makes me—

"Do you think she ever got—ah—*gets*—depressed?" This question doesn't sound smooth or planned. It sounds real. And Mercer's using the present tense. Christ. Is he actually *listening* to us? That would be a first. "You know, down and sad? Hopeless?"

Drip and I don't say anything to this, because yeah, sure she does. We all do, but we help each other and that's one of our private things.

"She did," Mercer says, no doubt adding up our silence to get his sum total. "I mean, does."

He gets more nothing from us, which I guess is another answer for him. "Would she hurt herself?"

"No." Drip sounds sarcastic and pissed off now, from zero to eighty in two seconds flat. That's how his engine runs, even on meds.

My mouth stays shut because I know I see different and I think different so maybe Drip's right and Mercer's question was totally stupid but—

Sometimes I don't think I can stand another second Jason do you understand that do you ever feel that way when everything goes dark and numb and you think you're never getting out of any of this and I put my hand over hers and feel how tight she's squeezing her locket and I tell her yes of course I do you know I feel like that a lot but you always help me and she says then help me now Jason please help me now and

—I see clouds. Nothing but clouds, black and thick and I want to scream and beat my way through them but they'll bite me and I'll bleed and I'll just get locked up.

"She didn't hurt herself," Drip tells Mercer. "Freak and I didn't hurt her and the sooner you *get* that and get busy searching for her like you should be doing, the sooner we'll find her."

A pause. Then Mercer asks, "Do you think we'll find her, Derrick?"

"You have to." He's yelling again, only now he's not mad and now I'm wanting to reach out and try to pat his hand like I did when we were little but we're not little and big grown Drip would punch me if I tried that. "*Somebody* has to find Sunshine."

I hear his tears even if he's not crying them, and if Mercer ever tries to mess with my brain and make me think Drip might have hurt Sunshine, I'm going to remember this and I'm going to know better because he's sobbing inside. He's wailing inside. I know, because I'm doing it, too.

And for some reason, Mercer's nodding.

"We've got a team going over her room and home, over her locker and classrooms, her family cars, and your school bus. Is there anywhere else we should look?"

Maybe he *is* listening.

I open my mouth to tell him. I open my mouth to send him down the path and through the thorns, to the river and the rocks and water, but the words don't come out and before I can make a single sound, Drip answers with a firm "No."

"Is this clearing important?" Mercer gestures to the mean dark all around us, and the mean trees, which I haven't been thinking about until just now when he points to them, thanks a lot, FBI man.

"We've been here before," Drip says.

Smooth. I'm impressed. But I'm confused. Part of me wants to tell Mercer anything and everything because maybe he's actually listening to us even though we're alphabets but a bigger part of me doesn't trust him and sort of hates him and I'm glad he seems to be getting closer to actually looking for Sunshine but I'm not sure I want a man like him to find her. I'm not sure I want him anywhere near her. There's something dark and monster and wraith about him.

"Don't be dark," I tell him. "She can't stand any more darkness."

"Freak, shut up," Derrick mutters where only I can hear him.

"What was that?" Mercer asks, and I don't know if he's talking to Drip or me, so I let Drip answer.

"He said it's dark, and we want to go back to the VFW."

"Okay." Mercer shrugs, relaxed like I'm not sure I'll ever feel again, and turns in the general direction of the VFW. He switches on a flashlight I didn't realize he was carrying, because he had it turned off when he snuck up on us.

He starts walking.

I don't know what to do and I don't think Drip does either because we just keep standing there until Drip finally jumps like he's waking up, then takes off after Mercer. I follow Drip.

Mercer lets us get a few steps into the twigs and loam and evil trees I don't want to look at before he says, "So, what do you two think about this Roland Harks character and his minion—what's his name—the little gangster?"

"Linden Green," Drip says. "And they're jerks."

Oops. There's that impulse thing. But Drip's right so I keep my eyes on his shoulders like I did when we were running down here and I walk and I don't say anything at all.

"Bullies," Agent Mercer supplies, and Drip gives him a snort that clearly says, *Well,* yeah, *idiot, what do* you *think?*

"Would either of them actually hurt somebody—hurt Sunshine?"

"Roland would," Drip and I say in unison, like we've rehearsed the opinion for years, and if you really think about it, we have.

"What about other people—like your teacher Mr. Watson?"

Drip laughs at this, but I don't, because the guy keeps giving me cases of the creepies, but why bother explaining. He's only doing his job, right?

Mercer's moving on. "Her stepfather—any issues with him?"

Drip's answering everything, so he says, "Nah, don't see him much," but I follow my Dad-ism about shutting my mouth rarely being a bad idea, and I keep my lips tightly pressed together on this one. There's something digging at me, something I'm trying to put words to, but it's making the clouds come back and my head's starting to hurt and my words, they're running away from me like Sunshine's words run away from her, and I wonder if it's because she's in my head and she's hiding the letters and periods and commas and even the thoughts, tucking them away and closing them up in her little gold locket so I can't see them or find them or say them out loud because I promised I promised I promised and I made the clouds and I gave the clouds fangs and they'll kill me if I talk because anybody who breaks a promise to Sunshine should die.

Mercer almost sounds relaxed when he throws out the next lure. "Her brother, Eli—he's interesting."

"Interesting is a good word," Drip agrees and I still don't say anything, because I agree with that, too.

Mercer stays quiet a second or two as we walk, and then he asks, "Is he a bully?"

"Sort of," Drip says. "Maybe?"

"Not really," I tell Mercer, and my voice still sounds off, but not as bad as it did when everything seemed dark and mean and scary, which it doesn't right now. I don't know why.

Because you're stupid. Because you can't see the truth any more than you can tell it. Truth is creepy and spooky. Truth is truth. You should always tell the truth, Freak.

"You sound pretty definite on that point," Mercer says to me, and I have to think a few moments to remember he's talking about Eli, and the fact that I said Sunshine's brother isn't a bully.

"Eli takes care of Sunshine," I explain, wishing I had a better way to put it. "He looks out for her. Sort of. When we were younger, he was a pain—but now, since he got back from juvenile—he's different."

Mercer lets this sit, and when Drip doesn't say anything, he prompts with, "Any disagreement, Derrick?"

"Nah," Drip says. "Eli's a dill weed, but not to Sunshine."

Yeah. Late dose of meds or not, Drip's tired. I get that, because my brain's misfiring like an engine about to throw a rod.

A strange sound bounces through the woods, and it makes me jump, then stumble. I bump against Drip, who doesn't stop walking, and it takes me at least three steps to realize the weird sound was laughter.

Agent Mercer . . . laughed.

Crap. Maybe the forest *is* about to eat us.

"I think I could come to like you, young man," Agent Mercer says to Drip.

"More than I can say for you," Drip says.

Agent Mercer actually laughs again, and he asks Drip if he's ever thought about going into law enforcement.

We leave the edge of the woods, walking into the park, and there's a crowd ahead, a crowd full of the colonel and Dad and the lawyer and Drip's mom and his brothers, and Drip's mom is crying and the colonel's holding her hand and they see us sort of all at once and sweep toward us like a flashlight tide, all talking at the same time—

"Where have—"

"What—"

"You found them! Thank—"

"What did you say to them? If no parents were present—"

"Derrick, I'm gonna kick your—"

And the colonel's got me, pulling me to her, and Dad's got me, too, and they're smothering me, and hugging me tight, and I can't hear much of anything and I hug them back until the colonel goes a little stiff because there's a new voice in the mix and it's a man, a strange man, and he's saying, "Excuse me, sir. I think you should get back to the VFW. We found something in the girl's room."

NINE HOURS

Agent Mercer leads the way back to the VFW, along with the agent who came to find him. Drip's on my right with his mom and two of his brothers, and the colonel and Dad are on my left. The lawyer's behind us somewhere.

We found something in the girl's room . . .

What did they find? Did Sunshine leave a note after all? The thought makes my pulse thump hard and loud in my ears. I want there to be a note. I want to know where she went. I want to know she's okay.

But what if she—

We round the last bend toward the hall, I almost don't recognize where I am. The VFW, it's—

This isn't the VFW. They're lying to you. This is somewhere else. You don't belong here. You don't belong anywhere. Belong is wrong. Belong is wrong. Maybe you should belong?

—The VFW looks different.

Trucks have been pulled into the drive—big trucks. And there are two towers on the lawn, one with two satellite dishes on the sides. Mist rises around big glaring lights that have been set up on the sloping front lawn, almost like spotlights on the front of the hall. Everything is so white-bright it's hard to make out the long tables lined with wide boxes, long yellow pads, and cups holding markers and pens. There's a person behind each table, and a handful of people in front—mostly folks from town with faces I know but can't name. They're signing the pads, writing their names on big white tags, picking out orange vests from the boxes, then lining up in front of one of three women carrying clipboards. The women seem to be dividing people into teams and giving them something that looks like a cell phone or a small handheld radio.

It's the government. They're here. They're here to get you, you freak, because they know all about you. Know and show. Know and show. Why don't you tell the truth?

My alphabet voices yell so loud it makes me blink. As we start up the main sidewalk, I have to work not to shake my head and work harder to shift my focus from all the lights and people and tables to Agent Mercer.

He says, "People are responding to the Amber Alert and our requests for volunteers. We're organizing a grid search of the area to begin at dawn."

"Maaaa-aaan," Drip mutters, his head swiveling like he's got ball bearings in his neck. His mother has him by the arm, which is probably good, or he'd be heading straight for one of the towers and trucks to poke at it and pull at wires and figure out how everything works. Drip can take anything apart. It's the putting-it-back-together phase that gives him trouble.

"You're organizing a search," I echo, not sure I heard Mercer correctly, but scared and excited all at the same time.

"Television, radio, e-mail, online social networks, highway information signs." He nods. "Everywhere we can send the alert and the requests, we do."

"Oh." Yeah. So, maybe I've been being an ass to him for no reason? Well, not *no* reason, but—okay. This is pretty impressive and more what I had been hoping for when the FBI got called. A search. They're going to search. We're going to search—with lots of people and some organization and maybe, just maybe we'll find her. We have to find her.

Tears pop to the corner of my eyes. I want Sunshine back so badly my whole insides hurt.

"I know it feels like we've been doing nothing but harassing you, your friends, and Sunshine's family, but that's not the case." Mercer sounds almost smug, but I ignore it because he's doing something and we're going to look for her and that's fine by me.

"Can we search, too?" Drip says, loudly. "Can we go? Now?"

His mom pulls him along and Dad comes around to my right to help her. When we get close to the front door, I see a roped-off area where arriving volunteers are directed until they go to the tables to sign in, and a big banner hanging on the VFW wall behind the tables reading SEARCH COORDINATION.

Everything seems too big and too bright and too sudden and too much and then we're in the door, into the VFW, and—

Even more people in here. New tables. Uniformed local officers. People with FBI identification badges like Agent Mercer's. We're standing on the edges of a pretty big crowd. I recognize kids from school, kids from class, and Mr. Watson with his screwball hair and calm-clown expression. I don't see Sunshine's mom or Mr. Franks, but I'm figuring one of them is here while the others are waiting at their place in case she calls or comes home. That bothers me a little bit, the thought of her getting home to just them and me not being there, but that's stupid, I guess. Home would be home. Just let her come home.

Roland's still in the hall, and now his pal Linden's with him. What was it Mercer called Linden? The little gangster? Fits him. He's lounging in a chair next to Roland's, only Linden's got his tipped against the wall, his dark hair in his eyes, chewing on something, maybe a straw. He has one person standing beside him, an older guy with silver streaks in his dark hair, dressed in black jeans and a black tank. He's fidgeting and glancing at the door like he wants a cigarette. Linden and Roland don't look nervous. They don't look like they have anything to hide.

It's you who needs to hide. You're a freak. You're a horrible freak. You know somebody was hurting her. You were hurting her. You hurt her, hurt her, hurt her. Maybe you only hurt her a little bit?

"You ever think it's weird that hard cases like Linden Green have parents?" Drip whispers, making me jump.

I shake my head, then rub my temples, wishing I could crush my alphabet voices or at least make sense of them. I know they're lying. I know they aren't real, but sometimes they sound so real and they feel so real and they say the stuff I'm worrying about.

You know somebody was hurting her. . . .

Do I know that for sure? Do I really remember that?

I know you've wondered everybody wonders why I don't talk much but it's better I don't say anything can you understand that because I need somebody to understand and you're the one who understands things Jason I know you don't show it that you can't show it but I trust you so much and her fingers twine around her locket and

"Yeah, that's bizarre," I tell Drip, but my voice comes out cracked and dry and I shiver because I probably sound like the dark, grabbing trees in the woods. Drip gives me a strange look and I glance down at my body. Am I turning into a tree?

Drip's mom yanks him away. Her expression has none of her usual tolerance and irritable sort of patience. She seems . . . wary. Maybe scared.

Why doesn't she want Drip talking to me? Is that real? Am I making that up or imagining it or alphabeting it? Maybe something's wrong. Or maybe something's worse wrong with me than usual.

I look at myself again. I'm still not a dark, scary tree. At least I don't think I am. Maybe Ms. Taylor is afraid Drip and I will take off again, but the VFW's turned into Search Central. No way we're going anywhere except out with an orange vest and a piece of the grid to explore.

Everybody seems alert. Everybody seems to know the FBI search team found something in Sunshine's room.

I lurch toward the murmuring, muttering, milling VFW crowd because I really don't know what else to do or where else to go, but hands grab me and I almost scream because maybe the trees followed me here but it's not trees. It's my parents and some part of my brain knows this but the trees still scare the hell out of me and I grab the wrists and hands and fingers expecting branches but when I turn I don't see black bark it's Dad and—

"Breathe, Jason."

I've got hold of his wrists. Both of them. I'm digging

my fingers in hard and my eyes are probably wide but it's Dad, not a tree, so I breathe.

"What are you seeing, son?" Dad's voice comes out calm and his face is calm, but his eyes—still not right. Not totally him.

"I'm seeing you," I tell him. *You and your wrong eyes.*

"You sure about that?" He's keeping his voice low, and I know he doesn't want anybody else to hear what we're saying.

I don't want to tell my father I thought he might be an evil tree, especially not with my mother standing right behind him looking as wide eyed as I feel, so I shake my head and wonder vaguely where the lawyer is, then go back to thinking about why we came back to the VFW.

"They found something in Sunshine's room," I tell Dad, and give the colonel a quick glance so she knows I'm talking to her, too. I try to make myself smile but I'm not sure it's working. Stupid alphabet. My father isn't a tree.

"I know," Dad says. "Captain Evans has gone to get more information."

Captain Evans. Oh yeah. That's the lawyer's name. But why is she going and not us? I let go of Dad's wrists, and he lets go of me, and I ask my question out loud.

"Why is Captain Evans getting more information? Why aren't we going?"

Dad and the colonel exchange a look.

Dad says, "Things like this can get tricky, son." He takes a breath. "It's best to leave the heavy lifting to the guys with the muscle."

The Dad-ism thunks against my awareness. Heavy lifting. Guys with muscle.

Tricky?

Dad's smile seems fake, which is something my father never does. Dad's always been real. Straight-up. So what—

Images of the trees blare through my brain. He could be possessed. Maybe the trees got him and—

That's not real, Jason . . .

Sunshine's voice. Just a whisper, something she's said a million times, and I always believe her even if she's not here right now because maybe she is, a little bit, at least in my head. My palm tingles again, right at the center, a locket-shaped spot like she's just pressed it into my hand to hold and banish all my bad thoughts, and I know I have to banish them on my own, at least until she makes it back to me.

Dad's not a tree, and he's not possessed by a tree. But something is wrong with him. There's that thing in his eyes, a glimmer of sadness, of worry I've never seen before, and it makes my stomach flip-flop. He could be scared and worried about a ton of stuff, like whether or not Sunshine's okay, or how the colonel's bringing the lawyer makes me look even more like a freak, or stuff from work I don't even know about—but I don't think that's it. He's worried about what they found in Sunshine's room, but it's more than that. He's worried—oh.

Oh no.

He knows, he knows, he knows, he knows, he knows, he knows, he KNOWS, he knows, HE knows, he KNOWS, you FREAK.

This time I look him straight in the face, and my words come out slow and very, very clear. "Dad, whatever they found in Sunshine's room, it's okay. I didn't do anything to hurt her."

Are you telling the truth? Because you're a liar. You know you're a liar. Liar, liar, house on fire. Maybe your house is on fire?

New expressions cross Dad's face, and I pick them out, one by one. There's guilt, then more worry, then . . . something like distance. Like he's stepped back from me in his head, and he's studying me like some of the FBI agents, who are watching us, all of us, and that's real and definitely not coming from my alphabet, but I can't care about the agents watching us right now.

"I didn't hurt Sunshine," I tell Dad, who doesn't react, but the colonel does.

"Of course you didn't," she says, forceful and definite. "That's why I brought the lawyer—so nobody tries to run over you just because they think you're an easy target. You wait. If the agents lean on Derrick even a little bit, his mother will hire three lawyers."

I can't stop staring at Dad and now I'm wanting to cry and I'm kind of wishing he was possessed by mean trees because maybe that would be better than realizing he thinks I might have done something awful to somebody else—and not just any somebody else, but *Sunshine*, for God's sake.

"Dad," I try again, ignoring the shouting and bellowing and moaning in my head. "How could you think I'd do anything like that?"

"I know you'd never hurt her on purpose," he says, trying to get closer to me, but I back a step away from him.

"On purpose? I'd never do it *at all*." I want him to hear me. I want him to agree with me. He *has* to agree with me. I can't have my own father thinking like an alphabet voice.

He doesn't agree with me.

My insides start a whole new kind of ache. I keep looking at him, waiting for a crack or a change or a shiver, for the moment he says he's sorry, that he knows I'm not that kind of guy.

Nothing. He's giving me nothing.

My chest crushes toward my heart, and I wonder if I'm going to die, because if my own father thinks I could hurt people, then who am I, really? *What* am I?

Freak freak freak freak FREAK freak FREAK FREAK freakfreakfreakfreakfreak . . .

The colonel's face goes red along the cheekbones and she glares at the back of Dad's head like I'm glaring at the front of it. "Johnson," she says, using Dad's whole first name, which is never a good thing. "You can't be serious."

Dad turns to her. "Not now. This isn't the time to have this discussion, Lisa."

"We shouldn't be having this discussion at all, ever!" Her bright brown eyes flash at him. "I can't believe you could—that for one second you could consider—"

She stops and I'm breathing hard and I realize some of the people around us have pulled back and folks are staring and three seconds later Mr. Watson's coming toward us with that all-is-well somber calm-down expression he uses when people fight in class. It's hard to take him seriously with his clothes all rumpled and his hair poking in every direction, but both of my parents go zombie quiet except for quick grunts of frustration.

"How are you tonight, Jason?" Mr. Watson asks in his most mellow voice.

Fine, I want to say because it's automatic, but it's not fine because Sunshine's gone and there's some lawyer flogging the FBI for information and my father thinks I'm a freak for real.

I keep my mouth shut. He's almost doing the stand-too-close thing to me, but not quite. Not enough that anyone would notice.

He's just doing his job.

"Jason's stressed," Dad says. "And it's past time for his medication."

"I'm not taking it tonight." I look to the side of him, because I really don't want to see his evil-tree face or his evil-tree eyes.

He thinks I could have hurt Sunshine.

Because you did, you pathetic waste of skin. You hurt her and you know it. You hurt everyone. Pain, pain, rain, rain, pain is all a game. I don't remember the last time I played a game.

"You most certainly *are* taking your meds." Dad glances at his watch, and the colonel—though her face is so different right now, it's more Mom than military—doesn't argue with him. Her I can look at. Her I can talk to, at least for right now.

To the colonel—to Mom—I say, "No. If I take my pills, I'll sleep for eight straight hours. Maybe ten. I won't be able to help find Sunshine."

Mom doesn't answer. Dad frowns, and Mr. Watson frowns with him. They can't exactly hold me and stuff pills down my throat, but I guess they could drag me to the hospital and force some doc to give me a shot in the butt. That's happened before, but only when I was already locked up in the freak house.

My right hip stings at the memory, and I remember how the dead-thick feeling spread out from the needle, down my leg and up my back until it beat on my brain and I dropped away into nothing darkness for hours, maybe days, I never can remember those times very clearly, but no way am I turning dead-thick now.

My fists clench, but I make myself relax and my fingers uncurl. My heart's beating too hard and I'm mad because it's not fair that I'm even having to argue this, that at my age I don't have any more choices or any more freedom than this. A guy should at least get to decide when going nuts is worth the risk.

"Agent Mercer says the first twenty-four hours are the most important," I remind Mom, more desperate by the second. "Nine of those hours are already gone. That leaves fifteen hours—less now—to find Sunshine, and I'm not sleeping through any of them."

Mom opens her mouth, but Dad jumps in with, "Taking your medication isn't open for negotiation."

"I'm not negotiating." Don't be obnoxious. Don't look at him. He's possessed by evil trees. No, stop it, there are no evil trees. "My best friend in the world is missing. The medicines work by blood level. I've missed days before, by accident, and that time on vacation. One day—even two—it won't make that much difference."

Dad goes quiet, frowning worse, and now his cheeks look as red as Mom's. She clears her throat, and I hold my breath, wondering if she's going to agree or disagree but she really doesn't do either because what she says is, "That's dangerous thinking, Jason."

And what I hear is, *she's hearing me*, and I relax the

tiniest bit inside until Mr. Watson comes out with, "We've gone over this in class, Jason. When you have an illness that's under control, the most important thing is not under-estimating it and getting lax with treatment."

"I'm not getting lax with anything." Somehow I didn't yell that. "I'm not taking fuzzy pills and letting Sunshine down. The second we find her, I'll take whatever pills you want. I'll take whatever pills anybody wants."

And Mom and Mr. Watson and Dad all look like they're going to say something but they don't get the chance because Agent Mercer comes striding into the room with Captain Evans right behind him. Four other agents follow, and they fan out toward Roland Harks and Linden Green, toward Drip and his mom and broth-ers, toward a room off to the side and when the door opens, I see Eli Patton inside. He gets to his feet as the agent goes in, but the door shuts. Then the last agent starts moving volunteers outside like cattle through a chute, fast and away, away from the people the other agents are approaching—like me.

Agent Mercer stops in front of me, and he glances from me to Mr. Watson and even gives Dad a quick brush with those cold gray eyes that seem suddenly twice as icy as the last time I saw them.

"We've recovered some clothing from Sunshine's room," he says, and waits, like he wants to see if any of us have anything to say.

All I can think is, of course they recovered clothing

from Sunshine's room. She's a girl. She has a great big closet full of lots and lots and lots of clothes, but he's acting like something is wrong with these clothes and—

I have to tell you something and she's got her locket tight in her fist and she's got tears in her eyes and I want to lift my thumbs and wipe the tears away and when I do she lets me and then she's got her face against my chest crying and I hold her and I want her to stop stop stop crying and the clouds are coming and the stabbing knife pain is coming but I have to remember even if I promised I need to remember but it hurts it hurts so much and I don't know how to help her until she tells me what she wants and I still don't know how to do it but I'll try and I'll do my best because it's Sunshine and I'd do anything for her even give up all my own books and games and movies I'd do anything for her even die I'd do anything for her even this and she's wearing jeans and a gray lace shirt with hints of yellow that make her black hair and black eyes look even darker and her pale, pale skin even lighter and I have to think she's beautiful she's so beautiful she's always been beautiful and

—Knives stab into my brain and my ears have to be bleeding and I'm breathing hard and the black clouds spin like tiny tornadoes in my eyes and

". . . DNA sample," Agent Mercer's saying, and the words don't sink in but then the knives go away and only my temples ache and the clouds stop spinning and I catch my breath and I think about crime shows and how if the police find anything with skin or body fluids on it test it and get DNA from it, especially when they want to see if the bad guy left some little part of himself behind at the scene of the crime, some little something that'll send him to prison forever, and my alphabet voices start screaming about prison and the rest of my mind starts screaming about the clothes and what they found on the clothes and what it might mean and whether or not it was the lacy gray-and-yellow shirt and jeans Sunshine was wearing the last time we were alone and from across the room where Eli's behind the door I hear a big bang and clatter like a table getting pitched against a wall and then I hear Drip's mom yelling about people being crazy and why are they even asking her boys something like this and Drip trying to tell her it's okay and he'll do it and Linden Green's father bellowing no f-ing way and how he's getting an attorney and Roland's mom is saying something like that and Captain Evans is mentioning it's a reasonable request and cooperation would be viewed positively but none of that goes all the way in my brain because what does it mean, what does it mean, what does it mean—

And Mr. Watson moves.

Sudden.

Fast.

He shoves me hard against Dad and we bang forward into Mom and Agent Mercer and Captain Evans.

I'm falling. I can't stop myself. Hitting mopped tile with my knees and palms and jarring so hard my teeth seem to crack and my vision shivers but I can still see him.

I can see Mr. Watson charging toward the VFW's front door.

TEN HOURS

My mouth hurts. My wrists burn and my knees throb and I'm somebody else as I shoot off the floor and charge forward, running faster than I think I can, than I ever have, and I slam into Mr. Watson before he can burst into the night and get away because if he's running then he's bad and he's done something and maybe he hurt Sunshine and—

And I taste copper and salt and fingers dig into my ankles and of course it's not me taking Mr. Watson to the ground.

It's agents in suits and three police officers and Dad's got hold of me. "Don't, Jason. Be still, Jason."

I wriggle for a second, wanting to get up and somehow jump on Mr. Watson and make a difference. Why is it never me who makes a difference? I pull out of Dad's grip because I want to do something—and I don't want him touching me.

"Why did the teacher run?" Mom's asking nobody, because nobody's listening to her and everybody's staring at Mr. Watson, who's howling and kicking and about to get himself Tasered or shot or at least punched in the face by the men trying to get him under control.

Somebody else mutters, "A room full of officers and agents and he's dumb enough to try a stunt like that?"

"I didn't do anything!" Mr. Watson shrieks. "It wasn't me. It wasn't me!"

My alphabet voices echo him like satanic parrots and for a few seconds I can't hear anything but that and for another few seconds I almost feel sorry for Mr. Watson but then Dad's pulling me up and we're standing and I'm shaking and there really is blood in my mouth and my tongue hurts.

Mom sees me wiping red trickles on the back of my hand and produces a handkerchief from her fatigue pocket. "Got all your teeth?" she asks in a low voice, and when I nod, she doesn't make a big deal out of it. She does have her good points, like not going ape over little stuff . . . and not thinking I'm a homicidal maniac like Dad maybe does.

That hurts too much. Can't think about that. I'm running out of space to store stuff I don't want to think about.

"Mr. Watson's weird," I tell Mom. "I've told you that before, lots of times."

"You have, but I thought—" And she stops, and she sounds guilty. I know why. Because nobody ever listens—not even our moms. All our opinions and instincts get ignored because everybody figures it's just a taste of our crazy.

"He's the kind of guy who'd think he could make it," I add, because he is. Mr. Watson definitely preaches beating the odds and staying optimistic and it doesn't surprise me that he thought he could run out of a room packed with law enforcement guys and actually make it. What surprises me is that he ran in the first place.

I mean, weird's weird, but running from the police? That barrels out of weird and does a boar's rush toward seriously creepy. And stupid. *Why did he run?*

For once, even my alphabet voices don't have an opinion.

Drip and his mom seem to materialize beside Dad, and Drip's mom asks, "What in God's name is this all about?"

"Got me," Dad says as the officers wrestle Mr. Watson to his feet and shove him away from the front entrance, toward some of the little rooms on the other side of the VFW hall.

That's when the door nearest me opens, and I see Eli Patton pop to the center of the doorway and grab the frame long enough for *PAIN* and *HOPE* to flash the room from his fingers. His mug-shot face twists as he watches what's going on with Mr. Watson, and his bristle hair seems to stick up double. I wait for his big ears to turn the color of bad apples like they always do when he's seriously pissed, but they don't, which strikes me as wrong, but it doesn't matter, and it doesn't matter what's really happening with Mr. Watson, it only matters what Eli *thinks* is happening.

He's gonna kill you. He's gonna kill all of you if you don't kill him first. PAIN *and* HOPE. PAIN *and* HOPE. *Run run RUN run Freak RUN and don't ever stop.*

The agent in the room with Eli is trying to talk to him. He's reaching for Eli—bad idea, don't do it, don't—

Too late.

My breath hitches when Eli surprises the agent with an elbow to the gut, and the agent goes flying backward, then Eli's running out into the room and straight at Mr. Watson.

"What did you do?" Eli bellows. "What did you do to my sister, you creepy bastard?"

Mr. Watson screams like a kindergarten kid and the agents and officers not fighting with him try to block Eli's path and blood hammers in my ears and all I can think is *no no no no she doesn't want this she would cry and cry and cry and he has to stop and we have to stop him* but—

Eli stops himself like he heard my thoughts or maybe he heard Sunshine wailing from somewhere very, very far away. His fists are still doubled, nostrils still flared, and he's got *KILL* and *DEATH* and *MURDER* written on his face sure as any of the real tattoos on his skin.

Drip and I both move at the same time, breaking away from our parents and lunging to Eli's side before any of the people in suits or uniforms can grab him. On impulse, I reach out and take Eli's *PAIN* hand. He starts to jerk away from me, then seems to process who I am. The wild-animal expression on his face flickers, and for two seconds, I see the boy version of Sunshine I've caught glimpses of now and then since he's been back from juvenile.

Something in him cranks down a notch or two, and I know he doesn't want to hurt me or be a jerk to me. She wouldn't like that. Sunshine would tell him to be good to me just like she'd tell me and Drip to keep Eli from having to go back to little jail or big jail, either one.

Drip follows my lead and takes the wrist of Eli's *HOPE* hand. Eli doesn't fight him at all. He's breathing like a bull sighting a matador, but he's not moving and he's letting us hold him back and—

My brother's not bad Jason he never was bad he's just had a hard time and he's got a bad temper and he gets lost in his anger but he doesn't if I help him so I have to help him we all have to help him and I know you will you and Derrick both because I love him and we can make a difference for him so he doesn't have to go away again because I want him home I need him home with me and

—The officers hustle Mr. Watson away, into a room, and get a door shut, and for a couple of beats, no one moves. My brain's spinning. My heart's beating so hard I'm surprised the sound's not coming through the ancient speakers wedged against the ceiling in the corners of the VFW. Everyone in the room lets us stand there in the center of a big staring circle, and Drip mutters to Eli, "Don't get in trouble. She doesn't want you to have to go away again."

Eli's palm is sweaty against mine and his muscles are iron tense as he glares after Mr. Watson. "She never liked that pig—and she knows people. Sunshine can read people easy, you know?"

I do know, even though I'm pretty sure she's been wrong about me, that I'm not the good guy she thought I was.

You know you're not. You know you're scum. The sooner you tell them the better. Truth is telling. Telling is truth. Why don't you tell the truth?

I risk letting go of Eli's hand. Nothing bad happens. Drip turns loose of the other hand, and we stand very, very still for three very long heartbeats.

"Son," a nearby officer begins, walking toward Eli with the agent Eli punched. The guy's not standing all the way straight, and he's holding his ribs as he hobbles. I see them from the corner of my eye, and I shake my head even though I know they won't listen to me but to my great big huge surprise, I hear Mom's colonel voice crack through the room.

"Wait."

Not a suggestion.

The men stop moving. Probably reflex from all their own military training.

Eli's gaze twitches off the door closing Mr. Watson away from him, and he focuses on Roland Harks and Linden Green, who have all four legs of their chairs on the floor. They're about fifteen feet from him, but it seems way too close as he lets out a rumbling growl.

"She doesn't like you, either," Eli says to Roland.

Roland's face does the bad-apple thing I was expecting from Eli's ears, but he doesn't say anything and neither does his big-mouthed mother.

Linden catches the next five seconds of the wrath of Eli. "You—you're just stupid, always doing what your boss boy Roland says. When he tells you to rob a bank or grab some chick off the street, you just gonna say yeah sure whatever and follow him to prison?"

Linden's mouth opens, but nothing comes out. Linden's father glares at Eli, and his muscles bunch. He's tense and ready, just like Eli, and that would probably be a fair fight. Mr. Green seems plain mean, like his son, but not as dumb. He's taking in the uniforms and suits, the enormity of the number of people who would jump on him and Eli both if either of them move, so he backs down with a dismissive grunt.

When Linden starts to say something, his dad smacks him on the back of the head and all we hear is, "Ow, Pop!"

Dad never hits me like that. Drip's mom smacks him sometimes. I don't think Sunshine's parents ever hit her but—

Karl will be here in a second to take me to the probation officer want us to give you a ride okay okay I'm just you know covering the bases and making sure everything looks okay don't get stressed

—Eli's words echo through my skull. Karl, Sunshine's stepfather. I can see him sitting in a car, looking old and lost and tired—but is that a real memory? I can't remember if Eli ever really said that, anytime, anywhere, but I think maybe he did and now I'm sure or at least I'm pretty sure that somebody was hurting Sunshine, that she told me that, that she wanted me to do something to help her with that, and I did, even though I couldn't figure how what she wanted me to do would help anything, and then she wanted me to forget it so I did.

You hurt her. It was you. You suck. Everything sucks. Cluck and duck and duck and cluck. There aren't any chickens here.

It *wasn't* me. No matter what my head says, I didn't

hurt Sunshine. I know I didn't. I never would. But when I argue the voices only get louder so I stop arguing and try to make my ears close but I can't shut out sounds that come from my own head.

"She doesn't want you back in jail, Eli." Drip's voice cuts through my confusion and brings me back to here, now, and right this second.

"Sunshine told me she needs you," I say.

Eli flexes *PAIN*, then *HOPE*, then lets his arms hang loose by his sides. He doesn't make any move to go after Linden or Roland or the door barring him from Mr. Watson.

"You giving your DNA to the Feds?" Eli asks, and I don't know whether he's asking me or Drip, but both of us answer together.

"Yes."

Twenty feet away, Roland and Linden squirm in their chairs, but their parents look sort of defeated, so I'm betting they'll be giving samples, too—unless they want to look guilty for refusing, or try the run-out-the-door routine that worked so well for Mr. Watson.

"I'm gonna do it," Eli says, though his voice hardens with each word. "But I think it's perverted, them thinking I could do anything to my sister."

"It is perverted." I point to the door hiding Mr. Watson. "But you never know about anybody, right? They're just being thorough."

Eli lets go a breath it sounds like he's been holding for an hour or two. He turns away from Drip and me, and he walks over to the agent he elbowed and passes him with a quick, surly "Sorry."

I watch his progress, feeling less than real, trying to make myself believe that the VFW and all the people in it are real, but everything's seeming flat and off and weird. I don't know if it's my alphabet, or how anybody would feel in a jacked-up situation like this.

Why did my teacher run from the police? Why doesn't Mr. Watson want to give his DNA? Who else is going to refuse?

"Do you feel real?" I whisper to Drip.

He gives me the stink-eye. "Freak, you sure you're gonna last a few days without those pills?"

Okay.

Not real.

I breathe to make it all go away, to make everything straighten out and line back up again. Then I twist way down inside because Sunshine's not here to tell me what's right and what's just my kooked-out brain. I wish I had her locket to hold.

I wish I had her.

How much time has gone by now? The clocks tick too loud. I hate them. I hate every second and every minute ticking away.

Did Mr. Watson do something to Sunshine? My gaze

shifts across the room to Roland and Linden. *Did Roland and his little gangster friend hurt Sunshine?*

I'm just you know covering the bases and making sure everything looks okay . . . Did Eli really say that to Sunshine—and if he did, what was he really talking about?

Eli would never hurt Sunshine.

Would he?

You never know about anybody—and *I'm* the one who just said that.

When Eli's safely back in the room where he's waiting for news on Sunshine, I turn back to my parents and Agent Mercer and Captain Evans and Drip's mom. My mom looks kind of pleased, and she gives me a nod like, good work. Dad doesn't look proud, but he seems relieved that all the fighting has stopped. Drip's mom looks relieved, too. Then she scowls at Drip for running away from her, and he scuttles back to her side.

"What's with Mr. Watson?" I ask Agent Mercer.

He gives me a single shake of his head. "Don't know, but I'd guess he's hiding something. People who have something to hide often try to run away, don't they, Jason?"

I hold back a groan. I am *so* not playing this game with him again. Whatever he found on those clothes, it's got nothing to do with me.

"When you find out what his deal is, will you tell us?" I ask.

"Maybe," Agent Mercer says, and I know that'll have to be good enough.

"How do I give you my DNA? Do you need to cut my fingernails?" I hold up my hand, aware I'm talking loud, but not really caring. "My toenails are longer."

But what if it's the shirt? What if it's the jeans she was wearing that day?

You're so dead. You're totally dead. Give them a piece of you and they'll track you forever and cut your throat. Float, float, float, float. I wish I could get on a boat.

"Ah, no." Agent Mercer's mouth twitches. "No nail clippings needed. Just—follow me, okay?"

ELEVEN HOURS

It's so detached and unreal and clinical when the technician finally shows up and pulls on her gloves, then sets a small stainless steel tray in front of me. There's a kit on the tray, and she opens the box, takes out two glass vials and two packages. She opens the first package and takes out a swab and gazes at me, waiting.

In the little VFW room with its wooden tables and wooden chairs and the single old light hanging from the ceiling on a slightly frayed cord, I feel like I'm in a television show. I wish I was, because then none of this would be happening—not for real, anyway. I open my mouth and the technician pushes the swab inside, missing my teeth but rubbing the rough material against the inside of my cheek. There's pressure, a little stinging, and she stops, pulls out the swab without hitting my teeth, puts it in the first vial, labels it, then opens the second swab.

This time I close my eyes.

It's somewhere around four in the morning, and I'm so tired and so sad I feel everything heavy in my blood, heavy on my heart, and stars dance in the darkness of my eyelids as she scrapes my cheek again. I drift almost instantly, to a blank, quiet place with nothing in it but soft yellow light, running water, Sunshine and her golden locket, and the peaceful scent of honeysuckle. It's like a fairy kingdom and she's the princess, and for once, I'm actually the prince.

It's not real, she tells me, but for once I can't believe her, because it is real. It's too real, and there's nothing even my alphabet can do to make it a dream.

Mom startles me awake when she rattles the table. I open my eyes, and she's leaning toward Agent Mercer, who is standing on the other side of the table from me holding a folder.

Mom growls, "How can he be a sex offender?"

Before Agent Mercer can answer, Dad, who's sitting beside Mom, says, "Don't they do background checks? How could they possibly miss something that huge?"

"He used a fairly well-crafted false identity," Captain Evans says. She's standing next to Agent Mercer, which seems bizarre. "The school's background check would have been benign."

"They don't use fingerprints?" Mom's tone is incredulous. "They don't check photographs?"

Agent Mercer shakes his head. "Not in your district. Not enough funding."

Mom sits back hard in her chair. "So anybody could plop down a set of fake credentials and get cleared to teach my child."

Captain Evans says nothing.

Agent Mercer says more nothing, which I take for *Well, yes, actually, that's exactly the case.*

From the look on Mom's face, I can tell some serious base resources might be shifted to investigating every educator in the county. If she could photograph and fingerprint every school employee in the whole state, she'd set it up tomorrow.

"Mr. Watson's real name is Burton Smith," Agent Mercer says. "He was convicted fifteen years ago, served two for aggravated battery of a child, then dropped off the radar after he failed to reregister following a move. That's when he assumed the James Watson identity. Probably paid a lot to get the documents of some dead infant—there are many ways to become someone else."

Really? I'd like to know what they are. If I became someone else, would the alphabet voices come with me? Even if they did, I might go for it, because I'm dreading the next round.

Did he touch you, Jason?

Was he ever inappropriate with you, Jason?

Did you ever see him touching your friends, Jason?

Because you know, us alphabets are all so stupid and unaware that we'd let some bizarre electric caveman-looking strange teacher molest us and never ever say a word to anyone. We've had all the self-defense-tell-your-parents classes, but we ignore those because we're weak and vulnerable and dumb and all that.

Trust me, if something bad's happening to us and we don't tell, it's because we have a damned good reason. Or we know nobody can help. Or we know nobody *will* help. Just like anyone else, right?

Keeping your mouth closed is rarely a bad idea.

Yeah, that has more meaning than even Dad realizes.

"Mr. Watson never did anything to me," I say before they can start with that crap. "He never did anything to anyone I know, at least not that they told me. He was just weird, like I said before."

Agent Mercer peers into my eyes for a long time, his expression completely unreadable. I can't tell what he's thinking. I don't even want to know. Finally he asks, "Weird in what way?"

"He'd stand too close to Sunshine and everybody, like he enjoyed making us nervous." I shrug. The sensation Mr. Watson created is hard to put into words. Just . . . slimy. A little to the back side of normal. "Sometimes he pushed Sunshine too hard. He was irritating, and kind of stuck on himself—but we didn't have that kind of problem with him. The touching stuff."

At least I don't think we did. If Mr. Watson had hurt Sunshine, would she have told me? Because she did tell me some things.

Did she tell me Mr. Watson was hurting her?

Maybe she told me everything, but I can't pull it out of my brain and I can't decide what I'm really remembering—what I know and what I might know.

Stupid, stupid, STUPID freak. That's all you are. That's all you'll ever be. Why don't you tell the truth?

"What clothes did you find in Sunshine's room?" The question just pops out. I don't mean for it to, but there it is, exactly what I've been wondering since Agent Mercer told us the big discovery.

Everyone stares at me. Captain Evans has her eyebrows raised. Mom looks surprised. Dad, of course, looks worried. Agent Mercer says nothing, and I can't tell what he's feeling, but my money would be on thrilled, because the freaky kid is starting to look guilty again.

"Why would you ask that, Jason?" he asks, and Captain Evans doesn't start arguing with him, and I can tell everybody wants me to answer.

Because I'm a serial rapist and I'm terrified you're on my tail. That's why I agreed to give you my DNA and sat peacefully while you had your flunky scrape it off my jaw.

Careful. I'm sleepy and tired and upset and no

meds, so I know I have to work not to get irritable and sarcastic.

Out loud, I say, "Because Sunshine is a girl. She has lots of clothes, so I can't figure out why finding clothes in her room would be a big deal."

"These clothes were hidden," he says.

"What do you mean, hidden?" Now I'm confused. "She's got a hamper in her bathroom, and a box in her closet where she keeps outgrown stuff she loves too much to give away. If the clothes were in there, they weren't hidden."

"You know a lot about her room and her habits," Agent Mercer says, his now-that's-interesting tone scratching across my nerves.

"I've known her since I can remember being alive. Of course I know her room and her habits."

"Of course he does," Mom echoes. "They've been best friends for over a decade, Sunshine and Jason and Derrick. They finish each other's sentences like triplets."

"When they were little, they had their own language," Dad says. "Took us forever to figure out it was pig Latin with a four-letter shift."

Wow. It's been years since I thought about that. Our magic talk. Or agic-quay alk-xay. I almost laugh. Then I want to cry.

Unshine-way . . .

Agent Mercer loses a little steam, but keeps his gaze

leveled on me. "Sunshine had a compartment in her closet. A place where she had loosened the boards."

My mouth comes open an inch or so.

Oh.

That, I didn't know.

Sunshine had a hiding place she didn't show me?

Why does that hurt my feelings?

And what was in it?

As if reading my mind, Mercer says, "There wasn't much in there. A small white candle, a well-worn picture of her father." He pauses. "A picture of you and your friend Derrick and Sunshine together. The clothing was wadded up on top of all of that, like somebody stuffed it there."

I don't say anything. I should be thinking about the clothes but the picture of her real dad and the picture of us together and the little white candle and—

We're graduating today and she looks all serious even though it's fifth grade and fifth grade graduation is stupid but we're going to junior high and she's holding her locket tight because she thinks it's a big deal and we all have candles because people aren't bringing guns and bombs and meth to school yet so candles are still okay and the flame dances in her black eyes and I wonder if the candle makes my eyes look better because I'm kind of caring if they look better because I want Sunshine to like my eyes and I'm starting to wonder if I like her that way but I shouldn't I know I shouldn't because she's my friend she's not my girlfriend but when she kisses me on the cheek she lets her lips stay longer than she should just long enough to make me wonder and she's holding her candle and I'm staring at it afraid to move my face because she might stop kissing my cheek and maybe I'm imagining she's staying too long and I'm pretty sure I'm imagining it until she finally moves her lips only she doesn't leave she's just whispering in my ear and what she says is I thought your freckles would taste like chocolate and then she laughs and I have to laugh and

—She saved the candle.

This time the tears come too fast to stop and spill down my cheeks, and I don't care about the clothes right this second, I couldn't care less. She saved the candle.

Mom puts her hand over mine. "Jason?"

I can't talk. I hiccup instead. They probably think I care about the clothes and maybe I sort of do, just wondering which clothes, but I really care about the candle, but all I can do is whisper, "My freckles don't taste like chocolate."

Maybe she was my girlfriend?

I'd give anything to hold that candle. I'd give anything to hold the locket. I'd give up my own life to hold Sunshine again.

I put my head down on the table, cheek against the wood, eyes turned away from Mom and Dad and everyone, and I cry. When my lids drift down, I almost fall asleep, then hiccup awake again as Mom slowly, gently runs her fingers through my hair and Dad's saying something about how long I've been up and how I won't take my medication because I want to help find her.

Agent Mercer and Captain Evans stay quiet until I can pull myself together again. Which I do. Sort of. Until I sit up and look at Mom, and I say, "I want her back," and start crying all over again. This time, Mom hugs me, and I fall asleep so fast I don't know what's happening.

A second.

Maybe a minute.

Then I pop awake and push back from Mom. "Sorry. I—sorry."

They know. Everybody knows now. Look at you. Look at how you're acting, you stupid freak. Freak, freak, FREAK, freak. . . .

Mom keeps her lips clamped together and lets go of me. Dad's staring at the table. Agent Mercer and Captain Evans are staring at me. After a few seconds, Agent Mercer says, "Do you have anything you want to tell me, Jason?"

"If you hurt the candle, I'll write the president and get you fired." Best I can do.

He blinks. "Hurt . . . the candle?"

"It's important. It's a good memory." I frown at him, then at Captain Evans, who's supposed to be my lawyer, but really, she's sucking at that because I don't think she's trying to understand me at all. "It's from fifth grade," I tell Mom and Dad. "From graduation, remember?"

Three heartbeats go by. It's Dad who comes up with, "The candlelight ceremony?"

"Yeah. What other white candle would she have?"

Agent Mercer doesn't let a second pass before he shoots back with, "Was there something special about that night, Jason?"

Like I'm telling him. Like I'm even trying to explain. "It was a good night, that's all. Alphabets don't get many perfect nights."

He waits. Thinks about this. Or maybe he's just hoping I'll get back to the clothes, but I don't. I won't go there.

Because he'll know you're guilty. What if it's those clothes, you freak? He'll crush you. They'll all crush you. Crush and smush and smash and crash. Why don't you tell the truth?

"When does the search begin?" I glance from Agent Mercer to Captain Evans, then at Mom and Dad. "How long until the DNA comes back and we know if Mr. Watson hurt Sunshine?"

It's getting harder to make my ideas line up. They're pinging back and forth and mostly staying on fifth grade and candles and freckles that might or might not taste like chocolate.

"We have our own mobile processing capacity," Agent Mercer says. "For a simple DNA match, we're looking at four hours, maybe five."

"And the search?"

"Dawn," Agent Mercer says. "But I'm not sure it's a good idea for you—"

I stand. "I'm going to look for her, and so is Drip. You can't stop us. Unless you arrest me, I'll be out looking for her with everybody else. Are you going to arrest me, Agent Mercer?"

He blinks at me again. I've surprised him. Well, good. Maybe he needs a few surprises. Captain Evans sputters for a second, then says, "Jason, I don't think you have to worry about that right now."

"Not until the DNA comes back, right?" I glance from her to Agent Mercer, then at Dad. "The three of you are so sure it's going to have something to do with me, but it isn't. At least Mom knows that. One person on my side's better than none."

Unless it's those clothes, and why would she have put those clothes in a hole in her closet? Shut up, shut up, shut up, shut up!

None of the three of them will meet my eyes, but Mom does. She says, "Why don't you take a nap for half an hour? It's at least that long until first light."

"Because I don't trust any of you to wake me up." To Mom I say, "Sorry, even you."

And then I can't take being around any of them anymore, and I leave the little room, and they don't try to stop me.

I walk out into the VFW main hall, and I'm surprised because it's still really full. Almost nobody has gone home, not that I can tell. Drip sees me, waves, and heads for me even though his mom tries to grab his arm. Over against the wall, Roland Harks and Linden Green are sitting with their folks again, in a slightly different place, so I know they got up for a while, probably to give DNA or for their parents to have "the talk" with them about Mr. Watson. If they gave DNA—well, that surprises me a little. If Roland did anything to help anyone else, it's only because he figured he'd get something from it somehow.

I let myself glare at him. I really don't like him. Maybe I even hate him. I don't want him out searching for Sunshine, him or Linden or either of their parents even though it's four more people because how awful would it be if poor Sunshine had to get found by them?

"I've been telling my mom Watson's a perv for forever, but she never listened." Drip sounds satisfied, kind of like I felt when my instincts about Watson got confirmed. That, and a little pissed because I know nobody ever believed me before he tried to bail out of the VFW rather than hand over his DNA.

"I told my folks he was weird," I say to Drip. "But I didn't think about him being—you know, like that."

"The agent said it's not likely he did anything to Sunshine. She didn't 'match his profile,' whatever that means." Drip shifts back and forth, foot to foot, foot to foot, and I know his second dose of meds is burning out. He told me before that the second dose, when he takes it, never holds him like the first dose.

I barely blink, because if I blink, I might fall asleep

where I'm standing. "Probably means he likes boys, or younger girls. Who knows. He's weird."

"I can't believe they took him out in handcuffs."

That image sticks in my mind. Our teacher, his hair and clothes all wild and frazzled, getting dragged away by big officers with grim faces. I can see it so clearly I wonder if it's hallucinations instead of imaginings, so I stop thinking about it and say, "Guess that's it with him, unless his DNA matches."

Drip goes foot to foot, foot to foot. He frowns. I hear the door open behind me, and I figure my parents or the lawyer or Agent Mercer's making sure I'm not running out the door or sneaking away or whatever.

"Eli's gone. They made him leave." Foot to foot. Foot to foot. If I wasn't used to it, it would make me even more nuts. "Mr. and Ms. Franks are here now. Eli's at the apartment."

I glance at the closed door where Eli had been, and I imagine Ms. Franks inside, Sunshine-older, with her dark eyes sad and filled with tears, and I have to stop thinking about it because the image makes my stomach ache. As for Mr. Franks . . . his Eeyore-sad face floats in my brain with its turned-down lips and its ugly mustache, and him I just don't want to think about, period.

"Did you know about the hole in the closet wall?" Drip asks.

My heart skips. "No, you?"

Drip shakes his head and I feel a little better, then feel stupid and guilty for that, because so what if Sunshine told Drip a secret that she hadn't told me?

But I do feel better.

You're an ass. You're a total ass. What's wrong with you? Freakspeak, speakfreak, speakyfreakyspeaky. Why don't freaks ever speak?

Drip stops foot-shifting and starts bouncing up to the balls of his feet, then back down. Up, then back down. He's pulling at the bottom of his shirt. "What do you think those clothes mean?"

"No idea." Unless it's *those* clothes.

Stop it. No reason it would be. She would never do that.

You disgust her. She probably left and killed herself because you make her sick. It's all your fault. Freak speak, speak freak freak freak. Freaks never speak when they should, do they?

Drip's going on about how it kind of hurt when they scraped his cheek. He says this loud, where his mom can hear, then drops his volume down to private levels again. "So, when the search starts, are we going back to our place?"

"Can't. Mercer will try to follow us."

"We can lose him." Drip actually grins despite everything, like he can see this in his impulsive little zippy-mouse brain, clear as anything.

"Drip, he's a trained FBI agent. How—"

"My brothers will help us," he says. "My brothers and Roland Harks and Linden Green."

I stare at Drip, and I can't help it, even though it's disrespectful and maybe even a little mean. For the first time ever, I wonder if Drip is crazier than me.

TWELVE HOURS

Just after five in the morning, the sky's the color of rain and dull metal and the air smells wet and heavy. Outside the front entrance of the VFW, cold sticks to my cheeks and arms and elbows like fog, and when I blink I see black reachy-grabby Farkness Biters out of the corners of my eyes but I know they aren't there, they aren't real, but maybe they're real just a little bit.

Stupid idiot. Of course they're real. They'll sneak up on you. They'll get you, Freak. Speak Freak freak-speak freak freak freak speak. Speaking wouldn't be a good idea.

Not Farkness Biters. No such thing. Those are trees. But there shouldn't be any trees this close to the VFW so they can't be here so maybe they really are Farkness Biters?

How long has it been since I had my regular pills?

"Everybody gave DNA," Drip's saying to some of his brothers, who have lined up to the right of us for the grid search. "Even Freak's dad."

"My dad, too," Linden Green says, and he sounds wavy and slowed like a Farkness Biter would probably sound, and I still can't believe I'm standing here with him and Drip and Roland, and we've got our orange vests on, and Drip's mom is on our left with Dad and two more of Drip's brothers. I think it's a bad idea but Drip swears we're cool, that there's a plan, that I need to shut the hell up or I'll get us all in trouble, and he'll explain in a few, when it's safe and he's finished blowing his nose.

"It's better if we all just go ahead and give samples," Dad says. "More efficient. The fewer questions and unknowns, the faster we find her."

Something needs to be faster. Twelve hours. Half the first twenty-four is gone. Whenever I look at my digital watch, my heart clumps with each blink of the colon between the numbers, marking seconds, tracking minutes—and counting down time running out for Sunshine.

"No more than fifteen yards between groups," the search coordinator tells us through an electric bullhorn. "The northern teams will progress to the school and beyond, to the county line. The southern groups will sweep the area between here and the apartment complexes, and stop at the interstate barrier fence. Eastern groups will cover the space to the city's edge, and the western groups will move until you get to the river."

That's us. One of the western groups—we at least got that lucky with the assignment, because the river is where Drip and I need to go. Drip's brothers are in the other western group, so they won't get in the way. We probably won't be in the exact right place, though. Who knows what team will actually end up combing across our private spot, and they won't even know where they are. Maybe they won't stay long.

Roland's got our radio, and we've been instructed how to use it to summon help if we find anything an evidence team might need to evaluate. Or if we find Sunshine.

We're going to find her. Or some sign of her. I'm going to hope for the best, no matter what.

We've also got our cells for backup, in case something goes wrong with the radio, and a central number to call.

We listen to more instructions, about staying a relatively straight course, and how often to call out, and stopping to listen for responses. We get reminded not to disturb or touch anything suspicious we find. Mom and Dad and Drip's mom all tell us to do *exactly* what the coordinators have instructed. Drip's mom adds a few threats to that, involving grounding, no computer games for a month, and wishing not to have been born.

Drip dances in place. I'm jiggling around, too. We need to go. It's time to go find Sunshine. I know I shouldn't get hopeful all over again. That's really stupid, but I can't help it because we've really got a lot of people and the daylight's trying to hammer through the metal sky and everything will be bright and obvious and maybe, just maybe somebody will find what we need to figure out what's happened to her.

Maybe we'll find her.

Some part of me knows that's not likely, but I shove that completely out of my mind.

We're going to find her.

The coordinator has us set our watches together, and gives us a time to report back to the coordination center here at the VFW. Then the search party surges outward, an orange squall line across the parking lot and the lawns, spreading up and down and backward and forward, everywhere I look.

"Sunshine!" I hear from dozens of places at once. "Sunshine?"

Men's voices. Women's voices. Young voices. Old voices. We're moving. Everyone's moving and calling, a whole orange storm of people.

"We're going to find her," I whisper, but Drip and Roland and Linden don't seem to hear me. They're looking down and around, kicking branches and rocks as we go, staring this way, then that way. Even Roland's calling out now and then, and he's using her name. None of that "pretty girl" crap.

Mom and her group pull away from us some, like

Dad and his group. Still within eyesight and earshot, at least until Roland hangs back examining a branch near the park. My heart does a big thump when I see what he's doing, and I crouch beside him, staring at the same spot while Linden and Drip stand over us.

"What is it?" I ask, suddenly breathless, but also frustrated, because I don't see anything but dirt and branch and leaves. What's here? Is it some sign of her? "What are you looking at?"

"Nothing, you stupid ass," Roland whispers, sounding exactly like an alphabet voice. "Just getting a little separation so this will work."

My eyes jerk to Drip, then I turn my head to glance behind me toward the VFW, where Agent Mercer and most of the FBI agents have stayed behind to be available if a team gets lost or in trouble or calls in for support.

"Don't do that," Linden tells me, kicking a spray of dirt in my face.

I blink as specks of mud and rock bounce off my eyes and cheeks and mouth, but I stop looking at the VFW. I wipe away the mud as I turn my attention back to the spot Roland's pretending to examine.

Mom and her group move farther away from us. I can barely see Dad's group now, and Drip's brothers went ahead of us into the trees. I watch the disappearing orange for a few seconds, and then I ask Roland, "Why are you helping us?"

He shrugs and stands. "Because I think maybe you *can* find her. You know her better than anybody else."

He walks ahead, through the park, toward the woods in the distance. Linden follows him like he's on a leash, and Drip and I trot along behind, looking pretty much the same as Linden. Confusion ties knots in my brain as I try to reconcile the Roland and Linden I've always known with two guys who would give DNA without much griping, and who would help a couple of lesser alphabets they consider prey. Help us outsmart FBI agents, no less?

What's wrong with this picture?

Just about everything.

But then in the last twelve hours, Sunshine vanished, my dad turned out to be one of the people who think I'm a psycho killer, and my teacher proved to be a convicted pedophile. Now the school thugs are trying to morph into hero material? If I wasn't already crazy, this might push me in that direction.

Don't go with them. You can't trust them. Don't be such a pathetic, stupid freak. Stupid is as stupid does. Stupid does as stupid is. Maybe you are stupid. Maybe you're not.

"Are you sure this is a good idea?" I whisper to Drip when he draws even with me.

I get a shrug from him, too, though he doesn't look relaxed or casual or sarcastic like Roland did when he twitched his muscled shoulders.

"Didn't have any better options," Drip says.

I don't exactly find a lot of comfort in that answer.

A few minutes later, as we get close to the trees, Drip says, "Get ready. Whatever they say or do, go with it, and then we're supposed to head on into the woods, this same direction, until the VFW people and the other searchers can't see us anymore."

"What do you mean—" I start, but right then, Roland stops, whirls toward me, and raises his fist.

I duck on instinct, but he doesn't swing.

"I should have known better than this," he says loudly. "I'm not listening to this crazy crap. Screw you, Freak. Stay out of my rearview."

Linden waits a beat, then adds a loud "Yeah."

"We're doing this my way," Roland says, still loud. "You head over there," he tells Linden, pointing over Drip's head. "I'll cover this side. Let the two wittle babies go straight down the middle like they're *supposed* to do. When we find her, they can watch as we get our medals."

"Hey, come on," Drip says, loud as Roland. "It's better if we—"

"Nothing's better with you." Roland pauses, laughs, and then stalks off, veering away from us into the trees. Linden heads in the other direction as instructed. I spare a quick glance at the VFW, and notice a couple of agents ghosting off as if to follow them.

Of course. The FBI would be expecting the bad guy to do something unusual, maybe give himself away. They've got a few agents assigned to watching or even tailing some of the searchers—like us. But Roland and Linden just divided them and pulled the focus off of me and Drip.

Smooth. Leave it to Drip to put together something decent on a second's notice. I wish I could plan like that.

I wish, for once, I'd make a difference.

And yet . . .

And yet something's bothering me. Everything about this situation still seems off.

Maybe a little too quickly, Drip and I head into the woods, straight-lining forward like the search coordinator told us to do, looking around and calling for Sunshine. In between shouting her name, taking a breath, and listening for an answer, I tell Drip, "This feels weird to me."

"Everything feels weird to you, Freak." He calls for Sunshine. Stops. Waits. He looks left, then right, and he says, "Come on. Nobody can see us. We just need to avoid the other search teams."

My heart squeezes in panic, but I don't know what I'm scared of. I look around me, half expecting evil trees, but it's daylight now, almost completely, and nothing looks that evil.

They're coming to get you. You know they're coming to get you. You can't hide from them forever. Farkness Biters. Biters, kiters, siters. They'll see you and get you and eat you. You don't want to be eaten, do you?

Drip and I dart forward, barely make a clump of trees,

and stand behind them while a group passes far to our right, calling for Sunshine. Way off in the distance, I hear Mom, and sometimes Dad, and Drip's mom and brothers, also calling. Drip calls for Sunshine, then we dash to a bunch of bushes.

This will never work. Somebody's going to see us. "What if Sunshine's actually in our grid and there's nobody to look for her?"

"Roland and Linden are covering it." Drip sounds annoyed. "Soon as they're sure the Feds are following them and not us."

We call for Sunshine. We stop. We listen.

"I don't see them," I tell Drip. "I don't hear them."

"They're covering it. It's how we planned it." Yeah, he's definitely getting annoyed. We're both standing against the trunks of trees, trying to blend in even though we're wearing neon-orange search vests. How stupid is that?

"Why do you think Roland and Linden will do what they said, Drip?"

"I don't know, okay? If you're that worried about it, we'll come back here after we search our place."

We run from the bushes to another group of trees. I see whispers of orange weaving through distant leaves. What if somebody has binoculars and sees us acting idiotic like this? "Maybe we should just walk like we went off course."

Drip glares, and I shut up. This is his plan. I'm not

supposed to screw it up. That's what Sunshine would tell me. She'd say that and—

Everybody wants to be good at something Jason you have to let Derrick do what he's good at and you have to do what you're good at and when I rest against the big rock wall under the tall rock roof at our private place and tell her I'm not good at anything that's when she leans forward so fast her locket hits my neck and for the first time ever she touches her lips to mine and I don't close my eyes and I don't blink and I'm surprised because her lips taste like softness and peanut butter and grape juice and I always thought she'd taste like stars and moonlight and maybe toothpaste but really how do you know how somebody's lips will taste when you're in sixth grade and practicing kissing the back of your own hand and when she pulls back she smiles at me and she says see I think you're pretty good at that and

—We stumble into the brambles lining the path to our place and Drip grabs me to keep me from falling. "Watch where you're going, okay?"

Thorns jab at my already-scratched ankle. The sting brings me back to the cool gray morning and I nod at Drip and he lets me go. "We're getting there," he says. "Don't call out anymore. Don't screw it up. I don't even know who's got this grid, so we should hurry."

My heart races and races as we plow forward, trying to go fast and not be too obvious never mind the orange stuff screaming look-here-at-us. We're doing the right thing but it feels wrong and I don't get that and Drip's not listening and I see darkness moving from the corner of my eyes and squeeze them shut. We don't have time for my stupid crazy brain right now. There's nothing there. There's nothing there. There's nothing—

Something hits me in the gut so hard I wheeze and pee all at the same time. My eyes pop open, feel like they'll pop out as pain riots through my middle and explodes out my neck and my face and shoulders and no breath comes and all I can do is pitch forward, falling toward the ground only I don't hit it because a foot whizzes up and catches my gut again, harder.

Stuff inside me cracks.

You're dying you're gonna die this is it you're dead Freak, dead dead dead and you can't do anything about dead.

My knees bash into the dirt and thorns and I puke a big bitter wad of the nothing in my smashed belly. Air. Need to breathe. Can't breathe. My chest is broken. My guts must be broken. My arms fold around my ribs and I'm trying to see who, to see what, but I'm seeing spots and stars and hearing a muffled *mmm-mmmm-mmmmmm* sound a lot like Drip trying to yell when somebody's got a hand over his mouth and—

"Did you think it would be that easy, you frigging freak?"

A kick lands on my ass, launching me forward, face to

the dirt right next to thorns, oh God thorns almost in my eyes and I wad up and keep my arms wrapped around my ribs because that voice—

That was Roland's voice.

"What the hell was that, back at the VFW, jumping me in front of my mom?" He's talking like a sad, sarcastic teacher, giving a lesson. "You dissed me in front of people. Did you think I'd let you get away with that?"

He kicks my back so hard and it hurts so bad I don't know how I'll ever move again and I can't see anything but dark because I can't can't can't breathe and I'm thinking how in books and movies bullies always cave when you stand up to them but those are bullies maybe just normal bullies not alphabet bullies with flat, dead eyes and flat, dead souls and he kicks me again and he kicks me again and I don't try to fight back because I think I'm dying but I don't want to die and it won't help. I'm prey, not a predator. I don't kick. I get kicked and Roland's saying, "Go on, Freak. Squeal. Cry like a baby. But if you tell anybody about this, I'll kill you."

Kick.

I barely feel it now because there's just too much pain so there can't be any more and I am crying but at least I'm not squealing so that's got to count for something and he's laughing at me but I really don't care about that because he's not kicking me again he's telling Drip that Drip'll die if he squeaks a single word. "You'll die," Roland says.

"You know I'll do it. The two of you—it would be like sticking pins in bugs."

I hear the sound of fist hitting gut, only this time it's not mine and then Drip's in the dirt next to me, holding his belly and moaning and Linden shoves him over so he falls in the thorns.

He's got his face turned away from me but I can tell he's hurting and he's crying like me but he's not squealing either even though thorns are poking into him everywhere and he's bleeding.

"Losers," Roland growls, and he sounds exactly like Bastard because maybe he is Bastard. Maybe all these years I've had Roland in my head. "Don't *ever* talk to me again unless I talk to you first—and don't *ever* touch me again. I'll beat your head in."

I don't move. I squeeze my eyes shut. The tears I can't do anything about. The wheezing I can't do anything about. I think I'm lying in my own vomit but that's okay because hey that's what losers, do, right?

Drip's not moving, either. We both know better. If we start yelling for help they'll beat us worse before anybody gets here—or they'll run away and wait and beat the hell out of us later. That's how it goes. That's how it is. They didn't leave any marks on our faces. They'll act innocent. They'll say we fell. Everybody knows how clumsy Drip can be. Or maybe he and that freak got in a fight and beat on each other. We weren't even with them, officer, come on. We fought with them and went our own way before they ever went into the woods. Everybody saw that, right?

Stupid freak. Such a pathetic freak. No hope for losers like you. Losers are losers are losers forever. Don't you wish you could be a winner just once a winner but can freaks ever really win anything after all?

Underbrush crumples and cracks as Roland and Linden head off, maybe to go back to the VFW, maybe to search, maybe to hide and wait for us somewhere else and finish the killing job. I keep still until I can't hear them anymore.

Sunshine . . .

Sunshine . . .

Sunshine . . .

Her name echoes in the distance, from dozens of different voices, in my head and out of my head and real sunlight touches my cheeks and heats my tears and I keep lying still because I'm scared and I'm a loser and I don't know what to do. Why does everybody but me know what to do?

THIRTEEN HOURS

I know sometimes it gets bad because it gets really bad for me but we can't let that stop us we can't let that kill us right because even though we're alphabets we've got a right to live we've got a right to be happy and I think we can be happy Jason if we try if we want to I think we can all be happy together and

"Freak." Drip sounds bad. Really shaky. "Can you move?"

I don't want to move. I don't want to stop thinking about Sunshine and seeing her in my mind and if I died right here that would be mostly okay because I'd be seeing her like this. I don't move because of that, and because I'm scared and a big coward and a huge baby and everything hurts and I'm lying in the dirt in a bunch of bile I puked and I'm afraid if I move somehow something will get worse.

"Seriously," Drip says. "Can you move or should I go get help?"

"No help," I mutter, and the air moving up through my chest and throat to make my words—that hurts. "They'll kill us. You heard them."

Drip goes quiet. Then he starts to cry. Then he starts to sob. Then I know I have to move, so I do and when I straighten on the ground to try to stand, stuff in my chest and middle crunches and I want to scream but I can't scream so I don't.

It hurts. I can't do this. But I have to do this.

Loser, loser, loser, loser, loser, loser, freak, freak, FREAK . . .

I manage to sit up and realize I'm sitting right next to Drip, who's crawled himself out of the thorns and his arms are bleeding and his fingers and his hands and he's covering his face and he's crying. His skinny shoulders shake from the force of it.

"My fault," he blubbers. "I'm sorry. I'm so sorry, Freak. I thought—"

My teeth grind against the pain as I lift my arm and get it around him to interrupt him. "Stop it. It's not. You can't help that they're mean."

"Shouldn't have trusted them." More sobs. "Should have listened to you."

"Yeah, well, mine's the alphabet nobody listens to, so that's not your fault, either—kind of like you're the alphabet nobody'll trust to carry their fine china."

His shoulders shake under my arm. Then they stop.

He takes a breath. I wish I could get a full one but I can't and I'm still seeing stars and tasting bile and there's kind of a whistling in my ears.

"Fine china?" he murmurs. He glances at me, his eyes bloodshot. "Seriously? That's the best you can do?"

"Fine china. Expensive electronics. You know, anything delicate."

"Screw you, Freak."

I manage to smile but that hurts, too, so I stop.

"I'll go get help," he says.

I shake my head then quit before something else in my body grinds or breaks. "No. No way. We got this far."

"Man, you can't even stand up. How are you—"

I force myself to my feet and somehow I don't scream or faint even if I'm not really sure how because it hurts so much. But I do it, and I make myself turn to face Drip, and I make myself look at him, and I make myself say, "We can't let her down. Let's go, okay?"

He doesn't say anything.

After a second, he just starts walking. Sort of. More like hobbling.

And so we move. Slow at first. It takes forever to gain ground because both of us are just limping. Both of us hold our ribs. If I move wrong, all I can do is stop and gasp and blink away the stars and tears, but I figure out pretty quick how to move where I don't kill myself with each step. We're doing it. Down the path. We're getting there. By tomorrow at least. Christ, this is slow.

And the sun's out full now, no morning clouds, and it's getting warmer, and we're getting closer, and there's the opening and the place we hide the shears we use to cut the brambles and we're through it and—

And here we are.

Our quiet place. Our special spot. And the river's still moving fast alongside it, still rushing over the stones all clear with foam on top, and there's still trees on the other side and the big huge rock hanging out across the river, and—

Sunshine still isn't here.

I think we both know that.

I think we both knew it before we ever came here, but we had to come. I can't say why. We just had to do it.

In the glare of daylight, her absence seems so huge and wrong it's unbearable. My eyes take in every inch of the place, side to side and top to bottom, and there's nothing here. Nothing of hers.

Nothing of her.

All the pain in my body turns into nothing compared to the pain in my heart.

Drip limps toward the rock, and slowly, like he's way sore, he crawls to the top of it, and he sits, and he looks down at the rushing water and he hangs his head, and I can see his hurting, taste it and smell it and hear it and touch it, just as hard and sharp as I feel my own.

It hurts so much everywhere, all over, inside and out, that I just bend over. Then I go forward, crouching, then crawling, until I'm under the rock, until I'm leaning against the big rock wall under the tall rock roof where we always hide when it rains or when Sunshine needs to be totally away from people or when we're scared of Roland and Linden and alphabets like them and just don't want to have to be afraid anymore. This is our private place within the private place. Our special spot in the special spot. I close my eyes and rest my head against the rock wall, trying not to cry out from the aches in my body, in my soul, and trying not to think about the fact that Sunshine kissed me here for the first time, and she tasted like peanut butter.

The last time she kissed me, she tasted like Sunshine. A hint of mint, a tingle of cinnamon. I open my eyes.

She kissed me. Last Saturday before she vanished. She kissed me and she told me things I can't think about because the black clouds and knives will come to kill me. She told me things I barely remember and I'm not sure I didn't make it all up, even the kissing and everything that happened after that.

Something catches my attention. Something in the ceiling above me, straight ahead of me, toward the river and the spot where light barely trickles underneath the big rock. It's small, the thing, but it's not rock colored, not reddish or gray or even green like moss. It's more yellow, and it's tucked into a little crevice of stone.

My heart stops beating, and for a second my mind stops

working and the world stops existing and everything, everything, everything in the universe goes still and quiet and nothing because the thing in the crevice, it's not yellow, is it? It's not yellow at all.

It's gold.

When I can think, when I can breathe, when I can feel the stab and sear of the pain in my bruised chest and ribs, I reach forward. My shaking fingers find the golden thing in the rock, and when I touch it, the metal sends cool shocks through my existence.

I gently draw Sunshine's locket from its hiding place, the locket she never took off, the locket she never would have left behind—

Unless she couldn't leave a note.

Unless she wanted to leave a message.

A message for *me*.

Hidden here.

Me, and only me.

"Freak?" Drip calls from way up on the rock, seemingly miles above my head. "You ready? We should get out of here. I think somebody's coming."

And my brain is spinning and spinning and I have no idea what this means, no idea what to do, what I should do, what I need to do.

What does it mean? How did she leave it here? When? And why? If I open it—but I don't even know if it opens. What should I do?

I grip the locket and try not to bang my head in frustration.

What should I do?

"Freak?" Drip calls again, and the locket tingles in my palm like it's done the thousands of times I've held and squeezed it, the thousands of times Sunshine's brought me back from the dark places I go—

She left it for me.

She wanted me to have it.

—I'm sure of that now, and I want to shout because she's probably alive somewhere and then I want to scream and cry because no, maybe this means she's definitely dead but I don't know why I think that, I don't know what to think, I don't know what to do, so I fasten the locket around my neck.

It's tight on me, and short, but my neck's pretty skinny and my rounded collar's pretty high so I can push the locket underneath the edge of the fabric so it's as hidden and secret as our kisses, as what happened between us before she disappeared. Hidden and private, like this place, and like those things are supposed to be.

I don't know whether to be happy or destroyed and right now I'm feeling both. I wonder about telling Drip about it. I probably should tell him, but it feels wrong. She didn't leave it here for him. She left it for me.

"Freak, I mean it." Drip's coming off the rock now, and I crawl out to meet him—slow—so I don't move wrong, and so the locket doesn't come out from under my shirt. It feels good to have it, to have this piece of her so close to me, to have it touching me.

When I stand, the sunlight hits my face and my eyes close and the heat washes over me, soothing all the hurts inside and out, but not that much, not too much and Drip stands there, too, just stands listening to the water and feeling the heat until we hear people calling her name, people coming this way.

Searchers.

Searchers who won't find her.

I resist the urge to lift my fingers and press them against the locket. I just want to go home now. I want to get the locket home and sit in my room and hold it and see if it opens, see if there's anything inside it, maybe something she wanted to say to me or something she wanted me to know. It's so small, there can't be much in there, but maybe there's something.

"Let's blow," Drip says, and he starts out of our spot, and I follow him. We're both moving like cripples again, and sometimes when I move my arms wrong or turn at the waist, daggers stab into my ribs and chest and I can't breathe right.

"We should tell them we didn't find anything," Drip says. Blood has dried on his arms. His mom probably won't flip out because Drip's always bleeding from somewhere, but you never know.

"*We didn't find anything* sounds good to me." Even though it's a lie. And with Drip full of bramble holes and scratches, *We were careful* won't fly, will it?

I wonder if Roland and Linden searched the rest of our area. They probably didn't. I wonder if they'll be at the VFW. They probably will. No doubt they told everybody we whiffed and they had to do all the work. If Mom and Dad are there, they'll probably be pissed.

"As long as nobody tries to hug me, we're good." Drip cringes midstep, and I figure he's pretty sore, and thinking about how one of his mom's giant bear hugs will crush him like a bad grape.

"Where is she, Freak?"

"I don't know."

We're at the clearing now, and we're through it, heading forward, heading out of the woods toward the park.

"What happened to her?" Drip asks.

"I don't know."

Yes, you do. You hurt her. You humiliated her and disgusted her and she ran away because of you. Maybe you killed her. Maybe you killed her. Did you kill Sunshine, Freak?

No. NO! Just . . . no. I wouldn't hurt her. I could never hurt Sunshine, never would hurt her in a million thousand years or even more than that. And why would I hurt her and stick her necklace in the rock to find later? That would be ridiculous.

You could have done that. You would have done that.

Covers your tracks, see? Liar, liar, murderer on fire. Maybe you really killed her.

If we weren't already in the park, out in the open, I'd slap myself because I did *not* kill her and if I could kill the alphabet voices I would. I don't know much, I can't say much, I'm not much—but I know I'd never hurt anyone, especially not her.

Minutes pass, and more minutes. We're walking more slowly than we should. Can't help that. It does get better as we go though, like moving loosens up the bruised muscles and aching bones. It'll be bad after we sit again, but we've been through this before, Drip and me, a few times. Alphabets like Roland, they never leave you in peace very long.

At least they never hit Sunshine. At least I don't think they did.

"Here we go," Drip says as we get close to the parking lot. "Look normal, or you know the parents will have a brain seizure."

And they will, too. And there will be tons of fussing and questions and all of that will take away from looking for Sunshine, even though I'm not sure anybody should be looking anymore, because the locket—

What does it mean?

I can't wait to hold it in my hand. I can't wait to open it. I hope there's something inside. There has to be something inside.

We climb the curb of the sidewalk and the step up hurts and I wince and Drip groans through his teeth but we keep moving toward the coordination area, where lots of people have come back and lots of people stand around saying nothing and looking sad and the women with clipboards are checking stuff off and taking vests back and yeah, there's Roland off to the side with his mom and Linden and his dad, and neither of them so much as gives us a glance.

Drip's mom is back, and his brothers, and a little farther away, I see Agent Mercer, and past that, Mom and Dad, and they're standing with Mr. and Ms. Franks.

I catch a breath and my ribs throb like awful and I almost shout. Seeing the dark Sunshine-hair glittering under the sun, it's almost too much to stand, even if it's not really her. I should go to her. Talk to her. Sunshine would want me to help her mom any way I could.

"Later," Drip says as he breaks off, trying to keep an even pace as he heads for his mom, radiating no-don't-hug-me as best he can. Drip's never been able to put on much of an attitude, but he's trying.

I'm trying, too, and probably doing horribly, just like him.

When I pass Agent Mercer and get closer, I can tell Ms. Franks is crying. My heart twists all over again. Mom looks up and sees me. She gives me a little wave and a sad frown and shake of the head.

No, I didn't find anything.

Dad's face tells me the same.

No, nothing. There was nothing.

And I want to say, I found something, and maybe I should say it, maybe I should tell them all and let them help me figure it out and Mr. Franks glances past me like I'm part of the scenery but Ms. Franks looks at me at first with pity and caring and then with wide eyes and then with narrow eyes and she bares her teeth and I stop walking because all of a sudden Sunshine's mother looks like a Farkness Biter and I'm not sure if that's my alphabet or if it's real but I think it's real because she's pointing at me and charging toward me and now she's screaming at me and yelling at the top of her lungs and Agent Mercer barely gets to her barely gets her arms pinned before she grabs me and maybe claws my face off and he's asking her what is it what's wrong and she gets one hand loose enough to point, to point at me and screech, "Monster! Monster! What did you do to her? Where is she? You tell me or I'll kill you!"

And when everybody gapes at her, her face goes red from fury and she points at me again, and I realize she's pointing at my neck and I look down and realize the gold chain has come out from my collar and oh, oh no, oh crap, oh shit, and she's yelling, she's yelling, she's yelling, "Don't you see it? Can't you see it? That *freak* is wearing my daughter's locket!"

FOURTEEN HOURS

Fight for Sunshine.

That's my voice, not an alphabet voice because I do have a voice of my own. I do.

Fight for her.

But I don't know how anymore. I don't know if I can.

The holding cell is dark and it's stone with a metal seat and it stinks like piss and bleach and maybe old molded bread and it's quiet because there's no one in jail here—except me. Mr. Watson's already been carted off to some big detention center, and I'm probably sitting right where he sat.

You deserve it you slime, you piece of trash, you stupid, stupid, stupid worthless FREAK. Freak is as Freak does, Freak is as Freak does. You'll always be a FREAK.

I have to fight for her.

It's so dark and smelly and the bars are so close and the alphabet voices are killing me or something feels like it's killing me and I hurt I hurt all over but I can't let go because if I fall into the darkness with the melty faces and evil trees and yelling screaming endless growling and insults and chattering and whispering and snarling I'll never come out and I'll be lost and she'll be lost and I have to fight for her.

Don't listen to the voices Jason I know you can do it I know you can focus there that's it look at me what you're hearing isn't real what you're seeing isn't real don't give in to it don't let it take you look at me Jason look at me and everything will be okay and

Nothing will be okay because I can't see her and I can't hear what she's telling me and my palm's tingling for her locket but I don't have it because they took it away from me. Chief Smith took it away from me and his men handcuffed me and they brought me here and half the town was following and yelling and it feels like a movie from the fifties where everybody wears cowboy hats and storms the jail and lynches some guy and I don't really care if they do because nothing will be okay because I don't have Sunshine and now I don't even have her locket.

My eyes stay closed. I feel like I'll never open them again. I'm sitting on the foldout metal bench thing, holding one of the chains that fastens it to the wall, and I'm tapping my head *plop-plop-plop* on the stones behind me. No pain from that. Not really. Just a bumping. Maybe some comfort. Lots of hurting from everything else. Hard to think. Hard to hear. Hard to breathe.

Agent Mercer comes into the cell with me. I don't have to open my eyes to know it's him. I smell his FBI cotton-clean scent and hear the measure of his stride and the soft squeak of his leather shoes and I know it's him when he sits beside me or maybe the alphabet tells me it's him because the alphabet knows things sometimes or at least it seems to or I think it does.

There's a click of heels and a waft of perfume, and the cell door closes. Another few clicks and still without opening my eyes I know Captain Evans is standing in the corner.

"This is ridiculous and you know it," she says. She sounds lawyerly. The noise of her talking jabs into the rest of the noise in my brain and I want to cover my ears but covering my ears won't help because so much of the racket comes from inside. There's no running away from what's in your own head.

"Does she have to be here?" I mutter, opening my eyes just enough to see fuzzy, dim images of her, of the bars, of the side of Agent Mercer's flat-line mouth.

He's here to kill you. You're gonna fry. Fry and die. Fry and die! You'll never get out of this alive.

I don't care, I don't care, I don't care. See? I do have a voice. I still have my own words. I can still fight for Sunshine, at least a little bit.

"She doesn't have to stay if you don't want her to," Agent Mercer says. "By the laws of this state, at seventeen, you're not considered a juvenile anymore. Like any adult, you can waive counsel."

The lawyer starts to talk but I ignore her like an alphabet voice even though I can't ignore the real alphabet voices at least not much longer. "Seventeen? I thought I'd have to be eighteen."

Agent Mercer pays no attention to her attempts to interrupt, and he says, "In some states, yes. In others, it's sixteen. In this one—seventeen."

Captain Evans finally makes it between our sentences with, "It's a bad idea to waive counsel, Jason. Don't do it."

My gut hurts. My sides ache. My mouth is so dry I can't swallow and every time I breathe, daggers stab into my sides. They aren't real daggers, only maybe they are because they feel like big fat hot steel blades. I've got tears here and there, but not crying yet. As long as I don't think about Sunshine—

Don't cry Jason please don't cry I hate it when you cry and I can't make you better and I tell her I hate it when you cry too and I stop I stop for her and she kisses my cheeks where the tears were and I wonder why I've never kissed away her tears before and

—Great. Now I'm crying. But only a little.

"See?" Captain Evans sounds like she's won something. "He's clearly distraught. He needs his lawyer."

Shut her up make her stop talking make her go away make her die make everybody die you should die you should die you should die!

"What about my parents?" I ask Agent Mercer. "Do they have to be here when you question me?"

"No."

Simple. To the point. That helps when the alphabet voices are so loud. He's quiet, too. Quiet is good. I don't want Dad in here because Dad thinks I'm bad. I don't want Mom in here because if Agent Mercer gets me upset with Mom this upset she might kill him and I mean for real because my mom's a colonel and she's had to kill people in battles with her bare hands and she will protect me no matter what, no matter who. She could take out a nonmilitary guy, easy. Plus I don't want her to cry and be upset. She's my mom.

"That's not—" the lawyer begins, but Agent Mercer cuts her off.

"There's no law in any of the fifty states that says a parent has to be present when a minor is questioned."

Her tone changes to mean shark but I'm not sure if

sharks talk and I don't want to think about sharks because then I'll start seeing them too and really, sharks I could do without right about now.

"He's in custody," she snaps. "He's not just being questioned. Don't mislead him."

"In this state, in custody or not, at seventeen, it's his call." Agent Mercer doesn't sound mean shark or annoyed or like he's won anything. He's flat. Like always. What you see is what you get with him.

Maybe.

Die die die death death death he'll kill you kill you kill you kill you.

Through the slits in my eyes, I see the gray stone walls starting to bleed and slide and split and nasty-looking plants come through the stones and fingers dead fingers and claws and no wait it's branches the evil trees the Farkness Biters are here and when I catch a fast, scared breath it hurts so bad I have to bite my lip not to yell.

Dizzy.

I close my eyes again.

"He's impaired and you know it," Captain Evans says.

Agent Mercer moves. I think he just shrugged like me or Drip might do when we've had enough of a really irritating teacher. "Jason seems competent to me. Has since I got here. I think he makes more sense than most people I've met in this town."

"Stop manipulating him," Captain Evans says, only it

comes out like a hiss and she's sounding like a snake and all my voices start hissing too. "You know he's diagnosed with schizophrenia. Plenty of records to support that. Anything he says to you will get tossed if you don't let me stay."

She's a snake she'll bite you she's trying to kill you you're gonna die and fry and fry and die and nobody will help you ever again because you're worthless worthless WORTHLESS FREAK.

"See?" I nudge Agent Mercer with my elbow even though I don't much like touching people when my head's this bad because my skin aches and frig when I move like that the hot dagger-swords in my ribs try to kill me. "Nobody pays any attention to what I want."

There's a pause.

Nobody talks. Nobody breathes except the thousand voices in my head that all breathe at once like monsters from hell and then they scream and roar and then Agent Mercer says, "Do you want Captain Evans in here with you, Jason?"

His question drifts through the black Hades burning desert of my head, floating around the voices and the evil trees and the sharks and for some reason, he's easy to hear.

Fight for Sunshine. Fight, Freak. Fight . . . Jason.

"I waive counsel," I tell them both. "I don't want her here. I don't want my parents here, either, or Chief Smith, or anybody but you." That was hard. Too much breath. Hurts. Dizzier. Everything in my head gets louder, louder, too loud to think to live to breathe to even die in peace. "I'll talk to you, Agent Mercer. Alone."

If I open my eyes, I'll see blood. The walls will be blood. Captain Evans will be covered with blood. Everything will be red. I keep them shut.

She's arguing. She keeps arguing, but Agent Mercer says, "If you don't go on your own, right now, I'll have you escorted from the building."

And five seconds later or yesterday or maybe tomorrow the cell door clanks and shoe heels smack on concrete and stone and the whiff of bleachy piss gets worse as Captain Evans whips past me and out and away and thank God she's gone. Everybody's gone.

Sweat breaks out on my forehead and neck and my palms. I want to puke but if I puke my ribs will shatter and I'll die. I think I'm going to die. I feel like a bruise. I'm a bloody bruise. A huise maybe, or a bruman. Some sort of walking human bruise. Bruman sounds better. I'm a bruman.

Agent Mercer tells the officers outside the door to the room with the cells in it not to let anybody come back until he says so. I half expect him to get a tape recorder, but he doesn't. At least not one I can see when I do open my eyes and have to see him there in the cell door, with all the blood raining down around him. He's covered in it and it's awful and now I can almost smell it too like hot burning copper like the metal pan I left on the stove when we got the call about Sunshine.

Fry and die and die and fry and fry fry fry the freak the bruman freak YOU FREAK.

Bloody Agent Mercer sits beside me again and I'm glad he's beside me because now I don't have to look at him, not full on and that makes it easier not to scream.

"Where's the locket?" I ask him because I'd give anything to see it smell it touch it get a tap of Sunshine's magic so all this might get better. "What did you do with it?"

"It's been placed into evidence," he says, and I swear he doesn't sound happy. Almost . . . gentle. But he probably wants to kill me. Or is that just my alphabet doing my thinking?

"It'll be analyzed, then stored until trial, if there is a trial."

I shiver. Feel cold. I think I'm dying. They're going to kill the locket. I know they will. But they can't. They just can't. It's all I've got left of her and the locket needs to live. "Does analyzing hurt it? Will it get torn up?"

I can't stand it. That can't happen. Don't hurt the locket.

Don't hurt me.

"No part of Sunshine's necklace will be changed or destroyed," Agent Mercer says, and I relax but not much because my ribs hurt and my chest hurts and I'm dizzy and the cell is still bleeding. Can't talk because I'm trying not to cry because I'm happy the necklace will live even if I don't.

"Jason, I have to tell you, some people might take your interest in that necklace as being obsessed with or protective of a trophy. Do you know what I mean by trophy in this instance?"

"No." Talking through my teeth because if I don't the pain will make me scream. It got so much worse when Chief Smith's men put the cuffs on me. My arms behind my back—I can barely stand it even though I'm not cuffed now.

Baby. Whiner. Pathetic. You're a loser. You're gonna die. You deserve to die. Won't you do the world a favor and JUST DIE?

"Some criminals—mostly killers and rapists," Agent Mercer says like he's a teacher in class and I'm a student, "keep mementos to remind them of their victims and the crime itself. Often it's a piece of clothing or jewelry."

I laugh. Can't help it. Then I sob. It hurts so bad, but I don't even know if it's my body or my mind or my heart or my soul that's in pain. I can't tell anymore. I don't know if I care. Everything I do to love Sunshine just makes everybody sure I killed her. Why is that? What kind of screwed-up world is this? Maybe I should die.

But
She
Wouldn't
Want
That.

"Sunshine's locket is special," I manage to say to Agent Mercer, then get a real breath. Enough of one anyway. So I tell him everything, how I saw Sunshine with the locket that first day I met her when we were just little kids, and how she squeezes it to help her when she's scared, and how she always uses it to help me hush my voices and get rid of bad things I'm seeing and thinking. "It's like a piece of her, don't you understand? She would never take it off unless someone made her, or unless she thought she absolutely had to—"

Can't finish. Out of breath. For a second the world gets black like I'm falling asleep but how ridiculous is that? I can't fall asleep. Sunshine is missing and the room is bleeding and my mom's face fell off when the cops took me and Dad's too and Drip's and even Drip's mom I'm pretty sure the people I love don't have faces anymore so maybe that's where all the blood is coming from.

Fight for her.

I still have a voice. I still have my own voice. And Agent Mercer's waiting.

I can't remember what I just said.

He reminds me, so I finish with, "She might take it off to leave me a message. And I think that's what she did. Was there anything inside it?"

"I don't know yet."

I don't think he's messing with me but he's probably

messing with me because he's the FBI for God's sake he's the government and—

He's gonna give you the electric chair. Maybe he'll hang you or poison you. You're not even worth the electricity. You're not worth the rope. Fry and die or maybe just drink poison and poison probably hurts. You deserve to hurt.

—I want Sunshine. I want her locket. Mostly, though, I want her.

"Will you tell me if she left me a message?" Don't cry don't cry don't cry. "Please?"

"Maybe. Will you tell me how you found the locket—and where?"

So I do. I tell him everything from the moment I walked out of the VFW room after the DNA sample, and I don't skip anything, not even how Roland and Linden double-crossed us and humiliated us and kicked the snot out of us.

Agent Mercer stops me there for a second. "They've done this to you before, I assume."

"Sure. Lots of times."

He hesitates. Takes a breath. I barely hear it over the shouting in my head and the raining sound from all the blood and I really don't want to look at the blood but if I close my eyes I might go black again and if I go black and fall out then how can I help Sunshine I hurt I hurt so much—how much time does she have left? Will she drop dead when twenty-four hours is over?

193

No. Agent Mercer just said—or somebody—somebody just said the outcome won't be good after that.

The outcome won't be good.

She's not an outcome. She's a Sunshine. I *have* to fight for her. I have to help her. Hold it together. Don't go black. But it's getting harder to breathe. Maybe the blood is choking me. I'm going to die.

"And you and Derrick never tell anyone that Roland and Linden beat you up?"

"Why bother?" I'd laugh, but that would definitely kill me. "They don't leave marks, and—" I stop again. Can't breathe.

Agent Mercer finishes the sentence for me. "And no one listens to an alphabet."

Just now he sounded sad. Might be the alphabet, but I think he was, yeah, definitely sad.

"I just want you to know I'm listening, Jason. I'd call you Freak like you prefer, but I think I'm too old for that. It feels disrespectful to me, especially since you told me Sunshine wouldn't like it."

He's messing with you just trying to get next to you don't buy it don't believe it don't listen you're gonna die you're gonna fry. Maybe he's going to poison you?

"I don't care," I say aloud and the room is still bleeding and maybe I'm going to drown now and that'll be better for the whole world and Agent Mercer is looking at me so I think then I say, "Sorry. Was talking to the voices. The ones in my head, I mean."

He looks at me. His face falls off. I close my eyes. Open them. The face is still gone. Just blank skin.

The blank skin says, "Do your voices tell you not to trust me?"

"Sure. And that you'll kill me, that everybody wants to kill me, that I should die or just kill myself. They say I'm worthless and I'm stupid and I suck, that I'm bad and that I'm awful." Breath. Gotta get one. Hurts. I'm drowning. I know I am. "They say I do everything, that everything's my fault—even whatever happened to Sunshine. But it isn't. I know it isn't." Breathe. Need to, but it doesn't happen. I'm going black behind my eyelids. I'm going blood and red and then black and I'll die. "I try to keep believing it isn't, but it's so hard because the alphabet voices tell me it is my fault all the time and they never, ever shut up."

"I don't know how you cope with that. How you're even talking to me right now when you're hearing other voices."

"And seeing blood," I tell him. "And you don't have a face. Sorry. But sometimes people's faces fall off."

"My face is still here, Jason."

"Okay."

Maybe it is. Maybe it isn't.

He's a liar. You're a liar. You're a piece of shit. You're nothing. You've always been nothing. Loser. FREAK!

"Your medication makes this better?"

"A little. I can usually tell what's real and what's not, but sometimes I can't."

Who's talking? Him or me? I can't tell. Did my mouth fall off? I don't want to look in a mirror.

"Are you all right, Jason? You look pale."

Eyes closed. Can't take it anymore. Going blood going black going dead. "I'm fine."

Fight for her.

"Why didn't you want your parents and the lawyer here?"

His voice echoes and chops in with my alphabet voices so it's like a bad record played backward it's demonic and it hurts my ears and I hurt I hurt I hurt but I have to help her I have to try I have to try I have to—

"Because they'll try to protect me and I don't need protecting, and it'll just slow you down. Whatever I know, whatever I can tell you to help you find Sunshine, I'll do it."

Time passes.

So long.

I'm dying.

"I believe you. Now tell me about finding the locket."

So I do. I explain to the bloody faceless man who's probably Agent Mercer where, and how, and what I thought when I saw it. I explain about putting it on, about wanting to go home and open it and see if maybe, I hope so, please, maybe, she left me some kind of message.

"Jason, did you hurt Sunshine?" he asks and it's like the knife in my ribs the knife that's killing me dead in all the blood and black and faceless people will grow mouths and eat me and it's over it's all over.

YES. No.

Fight for her, damn it. Do it, Jason. FIGHT FOR HER.

"I didn't hurt her." Wheezed it more than said it. Voice is going. "Do you believe me?"

More time. Quiet except for my head and the blood-rain and the thump of faces hitting floors probably nobody in town has faces anymore there will just be facepuddles and so much blood bloodpuddles.

"Yes," Agent Mercer says. "I do believe you."

"If the DNA isn't mine, will I be unarrested?"

"Probably. Maybe. I can't guarantee that. That part's not up to me—and the police and the people here, they're pretty worked up thinking you might have hurt Sunshine or even killed her."

I laugh and it kills me it finally does kill me whatever's broken inside me breaks the rest of the way but I get enough breath to whisper, "The freak did it. Always how it works in the movies, right?"

"Something like that."

And then he's not talking probably because his face bled away to nothing but then he is talking again and he says, "Is there anything else you need to tell me, Jason? Something nobody might understand, something nobody might believe, just because you're an alphabet?"

"Yes."

He waits.

I try to get my breath, and when I do, I tell him, "I think I'm going to die now."

And the coughing comes, the killing-me-deader-than-black-and-red coughing and there's more blood blood real blood red blood black blood raining in my mouth, on my lips. There's blood spitting into the jail cell to cover up the rivers of faceblood. I can't sit up anymore, Sunshine. I'm so sorry. I've got to help find you but I can't sit up and I can't breathe anymore and I'm so sorry, I tried, I tried, I tried, and I'm falling, and somebody's catching me, somebody's holding me like I'm little again, cradled in his arms, cradled against his chest even though I'm hacking and spewing blood and wheezing and it hurts it hurts so bad and somebody's yelling *Ambulance*—

And now he's bellowing it and shouting it and kicking bars with his foot as he yells *Ambulance ambulance get me an ambulance and get it right now!*

THE CLOCK STOPS

Thick
tongue

Dead

Dead

Dead echoes in my head dead echoes dead in my head dead echoes dead in my dead head dead echoes dead in my dead head dead dead dead dead

Nothing

. . . Pneumothorax . . . serious injuries . . . bad beating rib fractures cardiac contusion bruising extensive trying to keep his blood pressure up trying to hydrate him this medicationis

topreventsepsisnasogastrictubefornutritionjustforawhilenotper-
manentsorryjasonthiswonthurtmuch

Faceless nowords from nopeople Fuzzy

Arm
burns
Everythingbroken

Black

Nothing

. . . blood pressure too low—watch it don't let him yank the
tube!

Pain

armstieddown

Nothing

Floatywords from floatypeople.

Mom. *You'll be okay your lung collapsed . . . little*
infection . . .

Poison poison poison she poisoned you somebody poisoned you nobody has faces don't look don't look don't look

Dad. *More medicine. Maybe a big dose. Getting it straightened out, son, I promise and I'm so sorry.*

They're killing you killing you you're really dead and in hell and that's why the faces are gone bled away because of you because you're bad because you're a FREAK.

Drip. *Dude. You'll do anything to get out of homework and jail.*

Drip's mom. *Touch that chest tube again, Derrick Taylor, I swear to God I'm gonna lay you out.*

Drip. *Did you see that he smiled he really did smile.*

Drip's mom. *Boy you better get over here to me right now.*

Nothing.

Smells like alcohol. At least it's not piss. At least it's not blood.

Nothing.

And then . . .
People are talking.
I try not to listen.

I'm getting better.

I'm not sure I want to.

Nothing.

And then

My head's talking, but quieter. Thick tongue. I've had a whopper dose of fuzzy pills. Thanks Dad. Thanks Mom. I'm hooked to machines. I can hear them. I can feel them. But I don't look at them.

I hurt, but it's inside. Outside's numb. Fuzzy pills. Pain pills probably, too.

Nothing

And then

My body's better but it's like I fell asleep and dreamed everything bad and then started to wake up only I don't open my eyes because I don't want to because I know the worst part is it's been some time maybe a long time so the worst part is I didn't dream the worst part that Sunshine's gone that she's gone and while I've been out and sleeping in blood and faceless people and poison and there's a tube in my chest coming right out of my skin and I can breathe now but it doesn't matter it doesn't matter at all because while I was in the black in the nothing doing nothing being nothing—

Sunshine's twenty-four hours ran out.

ONE WEEK, TWO DAYS

"Arrested."

I sound flat. I feel flat on the top layer, the fuzzy layer all glued tight down by the fuzzy pills, but under that, I'm surprised and I'm shocked and I think I'm maybe even relieved.

Agent Mercer nods. "If I may ask, are you hearing or seeing anything disturbing right now?"

We're sitting on Mom's couch, in Mom's living room, in Mom's little base house at Fort Able, because he called right after Mom left, and he asked if he could come over, and I said yes.

Mom's place is as small as the apartment where Dad lives, only there's lots less white. Cream-colored walls. Green-and-brown carpet. Lots of green stuff— military green—everywhere. Even the couch is that color green, with the only brown being the leathery arm guards and Agent Mercer's brown leather briefcase beside the couch. It's shiny, like it's new.

I'm glad we're alone. I'm glad I asked Mom to go do something today and give me some time to myself. Mom didn't argue. She's trying not to fight with me because it's only a few weeks before she's deployed again and I have to decide if I'm going to try to live with Dad even though he thought I could be a murderer or if I'm going to apply to get into some group home or something. School's still in session, but I'm homebound at least until Christmas. So is Drip. Stress and all that—and there's no SED teacher yet, since ours is in the big house now. The pervert.

"You can ask about my crazy whenever you want, Agent Mercer, and no. Everything's a dull mumble right now. More meds because of all the stress and my injuries and all the medicines they had to give me for swelling and stuff. Steroids can make me crazier, so they have to give me more fuzzy pills for a while. That's why I'm talking slow."

And sounding like my tongue's two sizes too big because it sort of is.

"Will you have to take a higher dose forever?"

"Hope not." I hold up my hands. They shake. Tremor. Nice side effect of fuzzy pills. By the time I'm forty, somebody will probably have to feed me. "Great choices we get, alphabets."

He doesn't say anything, but I can tell he's sorting it

out. If I take no pills or fewer pills I get loud voices and bloody rooms and evil trees and faces that go boom to the floor—or I can take more pills, like now, and get mumbly voices and dry mouth and slow, thick speech and slow, thick walking and the shakes.

"I might gain about fifty pounds and get diabetes, too," I add.

Agent Mercer closes his eyes like he physically felt each of my words. When he opens them again, I notice they don't seem so icy anymore. Just gray, like his hair. "How do you feel about Linden Green and Roland Harks going to jail for assault and battery? Because it is jail, not juvenile. They're both legal adults."

I give this some thought and try not to listen to the frenetic whispers in my head that sound like *shooshyshuttershssshhhhhhshuttershooshy* because if I listen too long it might turn into words. "They didn't make bail, did they?"

"No. It's pretty high. And the judge already issued orders of protection for you and Derrick."

But not Sunshine, because Sunshine's not here.

My healing broken ribs and my healing bashed-up chest start to hurt, a dull, empty throb, and I don't know if it's real or alphabet or just . . . sad.

"You'll have to testify against Harks and Green, you and Derrick both."

"Not a problem. But you might want to put some guards on Derrick's mom and his brothers, because if they get hands on Roland and Linden, it'll be bad."

"Noted."

Agent Mercer waits. Obviously wants to say some-thing. Doesn't. Then he steels his face and here it comes. "Son, I came here today when you called because we're wheels-up tomorrow. Sunshine's case is passing out of CARD's hands and reverting to state and local agencies."

This hits me like a punch and everything hurts worse and tears pop straight into my eyes and I feel . . . lots of stuff . . . fuzzy layer and all. "You can't just go. She's not home yet. You haven't found Sunshine."

"I know that, and I'm sorry—but it's how things work, Jason. Thanks to budget cutbacks and regulations, CARD is a short-term operation."

"You can't leave." My words sound slurred now because I'm trying not to cry. All my green bruises match the green couch and now the bruises inside feel worse, too. "You're supposed to be the best."

"Obviously not this time." Are there tears in his eyes? I think there are. "I wish it could have been different. Of all the cases I've ever worked, I wish this one could have had a better outcome."

He's abandoning Sunshine. I can't feel sorry for him. He's abandoning me. How can I even stay in the room with him? But I do feel sort of sorry for him. That, and I can't seem to move. It's the fuzzy layer. The medication sits on my skin, in my skin, in my blood, weighting me like chains. I might as well be tied to the couch, which is why I don't hit him, but he's sorry. I can see that. He even says it.

"I'm sorry, Jason." Agent Mercer clears his throat. "For mistrusting you when I shouldn't have, and for being one of the people who never listened to alphabets in the past. But most of all, I'm sorry I didn't find your Sunshine."

It's okay. That's the automatic response that tries to come out, but I don't let it, because it's *not* okay. Nothing's okay. Maybe nothing will ever be okay again. The DNA tests cleared me. They cleared everybody, even that sleeze Mr. Watson, but his probation or parole or whatever got violated because he didn't register and he was around kids and stuff. He didn't go back to prison for hurting Sunshine. He went back to prison for being an idiot.

You're in the clear now, Mom told me, and Captain Evans, but they both stressed I needed to *stay out of trouble* and not *draw attention to yourself.*

Maybe that should piss me off, but it doesn't. I know Mom's just trying to look out for me.

"I've been doing this for decades," Agent Mercer says, "but I could still lose my job if I broke the rules. Do you understand that, Jason?"

"Yeah." I give him a look and realize it's probably a lot like Drip's stink-eye. "I mean, yes, sir."

He smiles. I think my stink-eye probably looked funny. Then his smile fades to another expression I can't quite read. It's sharp and intense, like it's more important than anything that I pay total attention to his next words, so I do.

"It's against the rules for me to share facts or even opinions and theories with persons of interest in a criminal matter."

Mumbo jumbo, some of that, but I sort of get it, so I nod.

"For example, it's against the rules for me to say something like, I think you might be right, that Sunshine didn't get kidnapped or murdered. I think you might be right that she left on her own."

O.

K.

Not what I expected, but fuzzy or not, my heart beats faster and my brain whispers louder and my hands shake harder and even my lips start to twitch.

"It would be against the rules for me to say that even though there was no message in the locket, it seems to me the locket *was* a message to you. I shouldn't tell you that if anyone can figure out where she went—or why she left—it would be you."

My mouth comes open.

I think my tongue is shaking.

Stupid pills.

Stupid everything.

Me. Me? He thinks I can figure this out? He's nuttier than me, and that's a lot nutty.

Breathe, Jason.

Sunshine's voice. Like a whisper, not an alphabet. It's coming from so far away.

Agent Mercer looks to the side, then looks back at me with his jaw locked, like he's pushing back a ton of emotion. "It would *not* be against the rules to say that it seems to me that she cares a lot about you, and that you care a lot about her."

"I do," I whisper.

Because she's everything. She's absolutely everything.

Agent Mercer coughs like he's clearing his throat, then plows forward with, "Her family's taking it hard. Her brother's hardly speaking to anyone, least of all us. Her mother seems to be crying every time she's in public."

He waits. Looks at me. Like . . . he's waiting for something. For me to get something? Piece something together.

All the army-green and leathery army Mom smells get a little too much as tiny black tornadoes try to spin in front of my eyes and the knives try to stab at my brain but the fuzzy pills make a wall, make a cushion and nothing too bad can get through except he talked about Eli and he talked about Ms. Franks and he talked about—but no wait he didn't did he? No knives. No tornadoes. I hold them back long enough to ask, "And Mr. Franks?"

Agent Mercer keeps his gaze trained directly on mine. "He's on a business trip. Might be gone for several weeks."

"Yeah, he travels a lot. Sunshine likes it when he's gone. . . ."

Pain.

I squeeze my eyes shut and let the fuzzy pills wrap around the brain knives and soften their edges. My thoughts buzz and snap and pop like something electric is trying to come through, something big and burning and real, not my crazy, not my alphabet, but maybe—my memories? My real ones, not anything I made up or imagined?

How can I trust anything I think? How will I know I'm not making it up? I don't have Sunshine. I don't have any piece of Sunshine. I don't have anything at all.

The knives melt away. The black clouds never come.

I open my eyes.

Agent Mercer sags, just a little, but I notice it.

"Give it time, Jason," he says, quiet, like he's breaking every rule he's ever known. "I think the right information will come to you. I think all you have to do is turn the locks to triple zeros and pop the lid, and you'll have what's most important. As long as people like you are trying to help Sunshine, she's got hope."

"I'm just a stupid alphabet," I whisper as everything inside me sinks because he's going. He's leaving, and he thinks I can do something. He's trying to give me hope, but really he's taking it because what can I do?

"You're anything but stupid, Jason." He stands, reaches into his pocket, and pulls out a card. "This has my contact information. You call me or e-mail me if you need *anything*. And I mean that. I won't let you down a second time, not if I can help it."

I take the card. Study it. See nothing but blurry because of the tears because he's leaving. The FBI is pulling out and poor Sunshine, she's got nothing but local and state agencies now, and a torn-up family and pathetic me. Tears try to ambush me again as I realize her birthday's coming up, that she'll be eighteen and if she's out there somewhere she'll be eighteen all alone.

She's out there. She has to be. Even Agent Mercer thinks she's out there.

Agent Mercer puts out his hand. I stand and grip it, even though I'm not sure I want to, even though my own hand shakes like an old guy's because of the fuzzy pills. "I can't help her," I tell him. "You know that, right? I never make a difference and I can't make myself be any different than what I am."

He lets go of me and stands very still, keeping those gray eyes pinned to mine. No coldness there now. Something like warmth. Something like respect.

"Some people are so strong, they don't need to change, Jason." His voice cracks a little on the next words. "They change everyone around them."

And then he goes. He just goes, out the front door, closing it behind him, and I sit down in a chair, facing the couch like he's still there, and I pretend he's still there for a few minutes because I need him to be there. I need him to help me find Sunshine because I don't think I can live without her.

My brain trips and stumbles over everything he said.

Give it time Jason I think the right information will come to you.

Eli not talking. Ms. Franks crying. Mr. Franks on his trips. I feel cold when I imagine all of this. Then I think about Mr. Franks, and knives, and black clouds, and I don't like him. I never liked him.

People never listen to alphabets.

I've been telling Mom and Dad that for years, and I told Agent Mercer, too.

And I stop. Actually breathe, and I realize . . . alphabets don't listen to alphabets, either, do we?

I don't trust myself any more than anyone else does.

I don't listen to *myself.*

I think all you have to do is turn the locks to triple zeros and pop the lid and you'll have what's most important as long as people like you are trying to help Sunshine she's got hope

His words flash through my mind like Sunshine's always do, when I'm not on such a whopping dose of fuzzy pills.

I wish I could find the locks in my brain, the buttons to push and the knobs and dials to turn to straighten out what *is* from what *was* and what *might have been.* Real and pretend and alphabet, it runs together like watercolors, and the knives and black clouds are always waiting.

I stare at Agent Mercer's brand-new shiny briefcase sitting next to Mom's green couch.

"Oh crap." I dive toward it and grab it. How long has he been gone? Can I catch him? I'm halfway to the door before I stop.

Before I freeze.

Did he—

No.

But—

No. I'm crazy as hell. I'm crazier than ever.

I raise the briefcase. It is new. Like, just-bought-at-the-store new . . .

Maybe . . .

On his way over here?

The locks, two of them, are set on 1-1-1, 1-1-1.

Mouth dry, hands shaking, I carry the briefcase to my room in the house at the base, and I place it carefully on the bed and—

All you have to do is turn the locks to triple zeros and pop the lid and you'll have what's most important

—And

0-0-0, 0-0-0.

I slide the latches, and the locks pop open.

I lift the lid, heart beating so hard it's making my heavy, thick head spin.

There's a piece of paper, like a list, inside. Two envelopes, too, both small and padded.

I pick up the paper, and it's definitely a list—names.

Mine's on there, and Dad's, and Drip's. There's Eli and Chief Smith and Roland and Linden and Drip's brothers and more. The words *NO MATCH* are hand scrawled next to our names, and I get it. Yeah, now I get it. It's the list of people who gave DNA samples.

I read it once. Then I read it again. Then the locks in my brain really do turn to triple zero, because I realize there's a name missing. It's scrawled on the back, *Karl Franks*, with "no compel at this time—Sunshine Patton likely a voluntary departure."

Meaning . . . the FBI didn't force the issue because they thought Sunshine probably left on her own, right?

I drop the list back inside, pick up the first envelope and open it. When I shake out the object inside, my eyes go wide and tears come right away because it's a white candle. It's the white candle from fifth-grade graduation.

My fingers close around it and—

I thought your freckles would taste like chocolate and then she laughs and I have to laugh and

—And I have a piece of her. One precious piece. Agent Mercer gave it back to me. He's trying to give her back to me, even though I know this has got to be fifteen kinds of illegal. He didn't care. He's trying to do the right thing, and the right thing doesn't always go by the rules, does it?

If he were here, I might cry harder. I might hug him. I might kiss him. I run to my dresser, take out a pair of socks, separate them, and tuck the candle deep in the toe. Then I run in circles, like a big giant idiot, looking for somewhere, for anywhere—and I stop at the bed, which has metal posts with these twisty things on top. I untwist one and tuck the sock inside the pole.

There.

One piece of Sunshine, at least, all mine and safe and I won't tell a soul because Agent Mercer shouldn't get fired because he's the best person I know right now.

Back to the briefcase, breathing so hard it hurts where I had the chest tube and I cough and that hurts worse but I couldn't care less because there's another envelope and I'm hoping and I'm praying even though I know it can't be, that it won't be but I tear into it and I turn it upside down, careful, careful, with my hand out, and what falls into my palm is . . .

One tiny huge small giant perfect magic . . .

Golden locket.

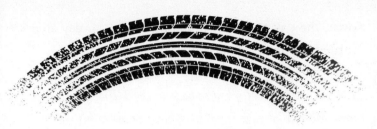

EIGHT WEEKS, SIX DAYS

What are you doing here Freak I mean Jason guess I should call you that 'cause if I call you Freak it would piss her off and I tell him I know you know something because your ears didn't turn red and Eli says I don't know what you're talking about and I say I know he's not on the list and the knives don't come and the clouds stay away and I yell at Eli that I know he didn't give his DNA and Eli says you better get out of here before Mom comes back because she still thinks you did it

"A road trip." Dad's voice crackles a little on my cell. "With Eli Patton."

"Yeah." I grip the phone too tight, but I can't help it. I can't help anything right now and I'm almost about to drool because I took an extra dose of fuzzy pills all on my own, the day after Sunshine's birthday, the day after she turned eighteen.

I'm not leaving, Eli, because back in the VFW your ears didn't turn red and he gives me a look but I point to his ears and say they always turn red when you're upset and mad so when Mr. Watson ran you weren't really mad were you because you knew it wasn't him and he says you're crazy but I say I'm not going anywhere because I know and I know because she told me and I know because the knives try to kill me whenever I think about it and I know because his name wasn't on the list and I know because she left me this locket and you know she wouldn't have done that if she didn't want me to remember

Eli's ancient Ford rumbles and bucks and shakes and belches, and every few minutes it slows down, then speeds up all by itself. The air in the cabin smells like burned oil and dead gym bags and I'm probably getting carbon monoxide poisoning and I don't care.

"Did your mother let you do stuff like that before she went back to the Middle East?" Dad asks, kind of nervous. He's been tense around me, but I'm staying at his place again, for now.

"Yeah." My breath curls out in a puff of chilled white air. No heat in Eli's junker. Could have figured that one, right? And it's November now, almost Thanksgiving, and cold as frozen snot. I've got on two coats and two pairs of gloves. "Mom let me be independent, Dad. Sort of."

Dad hesitates. Takes a loud breath. "Let me talk to Eli."

"No. I'm nearly grown. You can talk to me."

Eli gives me a sideways stare from the driver's seat, as slit-eyed as any Drip can fire at me. But he's also kind of smiling.

"Oh," Dad says. Then, "Okay." And I sort of feel sorry for him, which is all right because Dad's not really a bad guy. He didn't ask for a kid with an alphabet, did he?

Eli says you're not going to go away are you Freak and I say NO and he says you're never going to give up on this NO you won't let it go NO and he grabs my collar with fingers that read PAIN and HOPE and he shakes me but only once and then he says fine then come back the day after her birthday and don't say a frigging word to anybody you got me or I'll bash all your teeth down your throat you got me YES and PAIN and HOPE let me go and

"When will you be home?" Dad asks.

I glance at Eli, who mouths, *Tonight*, so I repeat that to Dad. Then I tell him it might be late so he won't worry in case we really are late.

When I hang up, I'm pretty sure I'm getting frostbite on my nose. We've been driving two hours already. I don't know how many more we have to drive and I don't ask because it's better if I don't know.

Why didn't you ever tell anybody why didn't you get her help or get him arrested or something but Eli looks away from me and he doesn't have to answer because I already know what he'll say I already understand he stayed quiet because nobody listens to alphabets and less than nobody listens to delinquents and if I really did want to die I'd hug him but I can't hug him even though when he looks at me I can see Sunshine in his eyes and

And two hours later, Eli's car slows down on its own and this time, it doesn't speed back up again. Eli fights the wheel and limps the dead old car to the side of the freeway, where it clatters and rolls and lurches, then stops with a way-too-final-sounding *ker-thatter.*

Eli and I get out. He raises the hood and does some serious swearing.

Then it starts to snow.

Thank God for extra fuzzy pills or my head would be a mess right now. Okay, so my hands shake like hell and my tongue's lead and huge and my eyes don't really want to stay where I put them—crap like this, I can handle. I think slow, but I think well enough to find an option, because the stupid car and the stupid snow, none of this is stopping me because I won't stop. I will not stop. Not happening.

Sunshine's locket seems to burn against my chest, safe from the snow and the cold, under my shirt and all my coats.

Nothing's stopping me today.

I pull out my cell again, and the card, and I call the number. It doesn't go to any kind of voicemail system or punch-this-or-that menu. It goes right to him and I'm so surprised I pull the phone away from my ear and gaze at it and Eli watches me, cold fog rising all around his head, mingling with the hissing steam frothing out of the car's engine.

"Jason?" he asks through the phone, sounding worried. "Is that you?"

"You said you wouldn't let me down again," I tell him. "You said you'd help. Now's the time."

It takes so long for him to get here. Hours. Four, then five. I have to whiz on the side of the road twice and it takes so long but he doesn't let me down and then he shows up driving a black car with government plates and we get in and the last hour is so quiet I'm not even sure I'm in my own head. There's whispering. There's muttering, but I can't really hear it and I can't really care because we're almost there. I don't know it, but I feel it. It's spreading out like a warm blanket, covering my legs then my belly and my chest and my arms and shoulders and even my face. I'm thawing. I'm getting unfuzzy. I'm getting alive.

We're almost there.

"Here," Eli says, and Agent Mercer turns off at the exit Eli shows him.

We don't talk. Not a word except for *here* and *there* and *left* and *right*.

Eli and I haven't spoken since I told him Agent Mercer

was coming to help us, to drive us the last part of the way and make sure we get there and make sure to do whatever we'll let him do and Eli started to throw a fit and—

He gave me back the locket

—And that's all it took.

"There," Eli says, pointing to a little charity-looking thrift shop and Agent Mercer turns in and I think I'm going to climb right out of my skin and I do climb right out of the car before it even stops moving and Agent Mercer hits the brakes and turns it off not even in a parking spot and he gets out saying, "Slow down, Jason."

But I can't slow down because this is it, this is where we're stopping and I'm opening the door and going in and there are rows of clothes and aisles of dishes and fridges and microwaves and the sign over the cash register says PROCEEDS TO WOMEN AND CHILDREN IN PERIL.

There are two women behind the registers and the nearer one sees me and then she sees Eli coming in behind me and her eyes get slitty and her face goes a little pink and she says, "Wait, you agreed—"

But the other girl behind the other register sees me and I see her and it's all done then and everything's over and I don't even try not to cry and she lets out a happy-surprised sound not a word because you know she doesn't really do words in front of most people but I'm not most people and here she comes here she comes here she comes and she's here and she's throwing her arms around my neck and I feel her through the numb and I feel her through the fuzzy and I know my alphabet will never block her out because no amount of crazy could ever keep me away from Sunshine.

She cries and she smells like honeysuckle and I hold her and she's soft and I barely notice that other woman as she shuttles us out of the main store and tucks us into a little closet with clothes pitched all over the floor, and she closes the door and I sort of hear her jawing at Eli and Agent Mercer's calm tones, maybe reassuring, maybe saying something stupid like, "FBI, ma'am, and I assure you, she's of age, there's no issue, all of this is completely confidential," but I don't care I don't care I don't care.

The room wants to gag me with musty old clothes and dusty old books, but I ignore that and a heartbeat later, the only thing I notice is the sweet, sweet smell of Sunshine. She's so beautiful, even in the light of the dusty old bulb hanging toward us from the ceiling.

We're sitting together on a stack of wrinkled shirts and jeans, and she's right in front of me, and I'm staring into the bright black of her eyes. Her hair's short. Cut and dyed with blond streaks to make her look different and she's wearing makeup she doesn't need with her perfect soft skin and the lipstick makes her mouth seem bigger when she reaches up and touches my cheek with her fingertips and says, "I knew I'd miss you but I never knew I'd miss you this bad."

And she tries to apologize for leaving and upsetting me, but I don't let her, and I try to apologize for remembering everything she told me even after I promised I wouldn't and for remembering what we—

But you know, it's hard to think past what we did, to think past touching her—

And she won't let me apologize, either.

"It's done now, Jason," she whispers, her words like rippling grass in my head, swaying and shooshing and soothing everything. "It's okay if you remember. It's okay if you remember everything."

I tell her about the search, about Linden and Roland going to jail. She tells me about how Eli found this underground network for her, how he scoped it out and got people lined up to drop her off with a woman who did pickups for Women and Children in Peril when things got too bad for Sunshine to stay home one day longer, when she just couldn't take another second of—

Of *him*.

Farkness Biter, my head whispers, only I'm pretty sure that's my actual voice and not my alphabet. Evil tree, evil bastard—whatever, it all fits, and I hope Karl Franks and his sad mopey face and his sad mopey mustache get eaten by something more terrifying than anything my crazy can dream up. No amount of knives or black clouds will keep me from knowing what he is now—total filth, not even worth the air he breathes.

"I couldn't tell you about leaving. I just couldn't." She holds my hands in hers. "It's the rule here. It's the deal we sign and if we don't keep our word people could die," and she tries to apologize again but I don't let her because it's okay, it's really okay and everything is completely okay now.

"Agent Mercer will get your stepfather," I tell her, wishing I could kill him myself and not go to prison and have to be away from her.

"You really think so?" she whispers.

"I know so. You and Eli, you might have to testify, but Agent Mercer will get him."

She glances down. Away. Then back at me. "You trust him that much?"

"Yes." And to prove it, even though she might not totally understand the full history of it, I slip the locket out from under all my coats and my shirt and I unfasten it, and I slip it back around her neck, right where it belongs.

"There," I tell her. "It's because of him you have it back. It's because of him that I'm here."

"No," she says, and she doesn't move. "Agent Mercer might have helped you, but I know if you're here, it's because of you."

She keeps her gaze fixed on mine the whole time, and my hands shake, and I'm pretty sure I'm not drooling, at least I hope I'm not, and I finally, finally manage to get the locket fastened.

The second it's done, she seems to relax into herself, to be even more Sunshine than she was the second I saw her running out from behind that cash register. Her fingers brush the gold of the locket, and a smile brushes the edges of her mouth.

"I knew you'd find this, Jason. I think I hoped you'd find me, too, even if it broke all the rules. If you trust Agent Mercer, then I'll trust him . . . but . . . I need to stay here for a while. They've got counselors and they're helping me, and I'm getting my GED and everything."

Oh.

Um.

Oh.

My ribs and chest aren't as busted up anymore, they're lots better, but it hurts again, all of a sudden. I had thought that if Mr. Franks went to jail, that she'd come back home, that she'd come back

To me.

But . . . that's okay, too, because I could come here, maybe.

"Can I—" I begin, but she shakes her head.

"No. Please don't ask. If you do, I might leave here with you and then—"

Then she'd always be an alphabet, like me. And she's not like me, not completely. She can get better—a lot better. And my heart twists and tears into tiny pieces but I tell her, "No. You're right. You have to stay."

A breath passes.

And a tear. Hers. Maybe mine.

"I'll come back to you." She touches the locket, and then she touches my face again. "I promise."

"You don't have to." I didn't want to say that but I had to say it and I have to mean it. It's the right thing, and this is Sunshine, and I have to do the right thing no matter how it chews me up and swallows me whole.

"That's what I want," she tells me, and she leans forward, and she kisses the freckles on my cheek, the ones that don't taste like chocolate. "When I'm ready. If it's what you want."

YES. But . . .

But . . .

I close my eyes.

"Sunshine, I'm not—I'm never going to be—"

"Normal?" She laughs. And then she says, "Good."

And then she doesn't kiss my freckles. She kisses my lips like she did before we—before we—

Before we were together.

The weekend before she left, when she told me she loved me, when she told me she needed me, when she asked me to show her just once, just one sweet time, that love could be soft and beautiful and right, and I showed her. It happened. It really did happen, it wasn't my imagination, and it was right, and I hope I was all she needed me to be.

She kisses me again and again, and in between the whisper-sweet, quiet-soft touch of her lips, I get my instructions, which go like:

Take care of Drip and explain all this to him if the bastard really does get arrested, but don't tell Drip or anyone else where I am.

Give your dad a break.

Make your mom help my brother join the army.

Graduate.

Pick a college because yes you are going to college because state schools have help for alphabets.

Don't study engineering because you suck at math so bad.

"Jason." Agent Mercer sounds gentle, almost like a dad when he comes to the door. "Son, we need to go now."

But I don't want to go, I don't want to go but I should I know I should and—

Someday somewhere I'll get there Jason I'll get better and I'll meet you along the way when I'm ready when I'm able it'll be okay Jason because you have a future and I have a future and somehow we'll find a way because we always find a way and

—And I can't pay attention to the last kiss, to the last hug, because that really would kill me but I listen to every breath and heartbeat and every word she says and I watch out the back window of Agent Mercer's car until the place cradling my Sunshine is nothing but a blur, then a speck, then a bright, soft place in my mind.

When she's able. When she's ready.

I push my fingers under my coats and my shirt and I touch my throat, touch the tingly warm spot where I wore the locket, and I'm scared and I already miss her, but I touch the spot, and I touch it again, and—

It'll be okay Jason because you have a future and I have a future and somehow we'll find a way because we always find a way and

—And I smile, because she's Sunshine—

And because she's Sunshine, I believe her.

∽ ACKNOWLEDGMENTS ∽

No book comes whole into life without many people working hard and making sacrifices. My family and my parrot stoically allow me to be absent from responsibilities and the world for hours and days at a time, my agent works on the contract, my editor reads and advocates and suggests (then tolerates my attempts at) revisions, copyeditors get involved, cover artists struggle to find the right image, marketing works on visions and strategies—and I know I'm leaving out dozens whose labors get even less recognition. Thank you all for your effort and patience.

Massive appreciation to teachers and librarians and bloggers and reviewers, who scour dozens of novels every month and talk them up to teens and anyone else who will listen. Books have to compete with movies, gaming, sports, music, and other entertainment vying for attention and dollars. Without advocates, books might fade into history. I hope the printed word will always have a place in society, and book warriors work to ensure that. You're the best, even when you hate my stories.

As for my readers, you're why I write, and thanks for reading. You know the real secret—that we're all Freaks at heart, and there's nothing wrong with that, no matter what anyone tries to tell you.